The Family Secret

The Family
Secret

Dr. Ralph Curtin

WIPF & STOCK · Eugene, Oregon

Resource Publications
A division of Wipf and Stock Publishers
199 W 8th Ave, Suite 3
Eugene, OR 97401

The Family Secret
By Curtin, Ralph D.
Copyright © 2014 by Curtin, Ralph D. All rights reserved.
Softcover ISBN-13: 979-8-3852-1560-7
Hardcover ISBN-13: 979-8-3852-1561-4
eBook ISBN-13: 979-8-3852-1562-1
Publication date 2/8/2024
Previously published by Lighthouse Christian Publishing, 2014

This edition is a scanned facsimile of the original edition published in 2014.

The Family Secret

ONE

Midmorning at the Plantation café was a special time for Pastor Randy and Laurie to discuss family and ministry matters before the daily concerns and the heat of the day set in. Drawing away from the house and meeting at the café twice a week was Laurie's idea aimed at having her husband all to herself with the goal of spiritual fellowship without the distractions generated by two college age children living at home. Yes, the workings of the pastorate along with family matters yielded both good and bad times, but in the end it brought them closer together. The purpose and direction of the church would be continuously discussed with passionate resolutions emerging. They were on the same page in ministry.

Over the years the emotional and physical demands of ministry, raising the children, and housekeeping—while finishing up her undergraduate degree—brought times of real conflict to Laurie and the family. Trying to prioritize without any help caused chaos at best. To Laurie, a man can be called of God to lead a church, but not at the expense of his wife and children. They had to come first after God. To Randy, this was a hard lesson he had to learn, nearly at the expense of his marriage. But that was behind them now. Plantation Gate church was expanding rapidly and now that Sean and Tiffany were young adults in college and the homeless ministry Laurie started at the church was doing well, they could spend some quality time together. They could kick back and enjoy the fruits of their labors. Or so they hoped.

Randy walked to the counter and ordered a skinny latte for Laurie and a tall caramel macchiato with a slice of pumpkin bread for himself and then shot a look at his watch. It was 10:30 A.M. *Still have plenty of time*, he thought, to chat with the Mrs. and then get to the church to oversee the completion of the building program. God is really blessing!

Redeemed how I love to proclaim it… played on his cell phone. "You're cell phone Pastor Randy!" the coffee technician yelled out with a chuckle. It seems pastor Randy and Laurie were regular customers and everyone knew of his iPhone ringtone. Randy answered the call.

Moments later to Laurie: "That was the construction foreman at the church. The new chairs for the new sanctuary have arrived. I have to sign off on the delivery. Catch you later." Laurie nodded in understanding and then threw him a kiss.

"Doing some food shopping then I'll call you," she replied as he walked off. Seconds later with his caramel macchiato in hand he was out the café door, leaving the skinny latte and the pumpkin bread with Laurie.

* * *

Once in the car his mind drifted into church matters. Budget overruns and construction delays were something he hated to deal with. This was why he handed the task to

Mike Rice, his administrative pastor. This way he could concentrate on developing the spiritual life in his church, something that both Laurie and he said he was good at. Yes, he would promote the building fund and oversee the bank financing, but after that Mike and the trustees would be in charge.

His cell phone chimed with a text message.

He stopped at a traffic light then unsnapped the I Phone from his belt and looked at the message. It was from Sean: *Dad, I've had a minor car accident on the way home from school. Come and get me at the corner of I-595 and Nob Hill Road. Don't tell mom.*

Accident. Not hurt? Praise God, he thought. *'Don't tell mom'?* What's up with that?

He made a quick turn.

* * *

Troubling thoughts cascaded into his mind as he drove to the accident site. Slightly foreboding thoughts that reminded Randy that there were areas in both of their children's lives that were hidden from view. Things were no longer the same as when they were in elementary school and high school when a tighter reign on their activities was possible. Now with driving privileges and an unchaperoned nightlife within the environment of a community college in the mix, the lure of the world can at times overpower spiritual and moral convictions. Even a pastor's son was not immune from such temptations.

It took only eleven minutes to traverse the distance.

"Oh, great!" he exclaimed aloud as he drove up to the scene. Sean stood leaning against his compact car with its front wheel sunk in what looked like a ditch that was part of a construction site.

"Sorry about this, dad," Sean said, real casual, laid-back. He pointed to the wheel then to the construction barricades and added, "Didn't see this when I made the turn."

Randy made a quick assessment and realized Sean was not hurt. He placed his hand on his shoulder and said, "Most important, you're okay." He bent over and closely examined the damaged wheel and continued: "We can fix this. The tire and axle appears to be okay. I'll pull you out." With that Randy went back to his SUV, opened the tailgate and within seconds pulled out a fifteen-foot heavy-duty chain from his emergency kit and attached the hook on the chain to the rear frame of Sean's car and placed the other end on the tow-hook on his SUV's frame.

"What can I do?" Sean asked.

"You get in my car, I'll work yours. On my signal, you put my SUV in reverse and I'll pull yours out." Randy reminded himself that his second year college son was not that mechanically inclined; excelling in academic prowess to offset this handicap.

Sean blinked several times then nodded. "Got it," he said and lumbered to his father's vehicle and slid into the driver's seat.

Randy opened Sean's car door to confirm the transmission's Park position and took a quick survey of the interior. Sean's books were out of his backpack and were strewn over the back seat with an empty beer can peeking out from under the passenger's seat. *And what is that smell?* he wondered. His mind went into overdrive as hunches formed. *This is not good.*

After he started Sean's car engine, he placed the gearshift in neutral and held the steering wheel firmly with one hand and signaled Sean with the other. "Pull me out!" he shouted through the window. Then he placed the transmission in Reverse and hit the gas.

Randy's SUV weighed nearly 1,000 pounds more than Sean's compact and with two more cylinders to boost engine power, easily hauled Sean's car out of the ditch. Leaving the engine running, Randy turned to leave Sean's car then glanced down at the ashtray. *Ashes*? He paused then took several whiffs of the cabin air and then shook his head. *This is not good*, he repeated.

"Nice work, dad!" Sean said as he approached his father. He patted him on the back and added in somewhat garbled tones, "I didn't want to upset mom with this. Thanks for rescuing me."

Randy motioned to Sean to put on his car's flashers and walk with him away from the traffic lanes. Once away from the sound of the traffic he said, "You didn't want to upset your mother because---" he paused to point to the car and added,"… because you've been drinking, right? What's with the beer?"

Sean took a deep breath and shook his head. "No big deal, dad. I just finished a big exam and needed to take the edge off. That's all. I only had one. No big deal."

"Are you able to drive now?" Randy asked sharply. "Remember, you're expected at the church now to help out with the youth group."

Sean gave him thumbs up. "I'm fine."

"No drinking and driving, Sean!" Randy snapped. "Are we clear!?"

With a scolded look: "Clear."

Randy looked down to the ground and silently walked away. He shook his head once more as he stowed the towing chain then left the scene for the church leaving Sean to his own deliberations.

* * *

The short drive to the church office seemed long. Niggling thoughts of his son's awkward behavior along with multiple questions began to haunt him. His breath smelled funny. He didn't seem focused. He didn't seem overly concerned about the accident. Several 'what ifs' lingered in his mind as well. What if those ashes in his ashtray were from Sean and not one of his friends smoking 'funny' cigarettes? What if he's hiding something from us? No, he doesn't smoke regular cigarettes. What if he's on something? Weed? Ruminations led to disturbing reminders. He remembered reading in his counseling book that 'weed' or marijuana is often cited as a 'gateway' drug that leads to harder, more illicit drug use. The text cited numerous facts that illegal drugs are being abused in epidemic proportions on college campuses.

No! he demanded of himself. *My son is a Christian!* This was not something that would define his family or his ministry. Nothing more than a one-time event in the life of the fanciful youth!

If need be he would deal with this at another time more forcefully.

* * *

Randy drove into the church parking lot and quickly focused on the group of men unloading the new portable chairs from a forty-seven foot trailer truck. He parked his SUV then walked to the foreman who stood with clipboard in hand checking off the cartons as they were unloaded. "So far, so good Pastor Randy," he said.

"How many so far, Louie?" Randy replied with a nod.

Louie the truck driver pointed to the next carton being wheeled away on the dolly and said, "That makes 300."

Randy did a quick calculation as his executive pastor, Mike, walked up. "Okay, two hundred to go." Mike was more than his administrative pastor, as a strong conservative Christian he was a loyal partner and friend that supported the senior pastor's vision casting and expansion project.

"They look real good inside, especially with the new carpet, Randy," Mike said with a wink.

Randy knew historically that the choice of color and style of the carpet brought many churches to the brink of splitting. It always annoyed him that differences of theology and doctrine were something that many church members seemed to overlook or compromise on, but one thing they would not tolerate was the clashing of carpet with the color of the walls. Fortunately his trustees, deacons and congregation all agreed on the changes. "That's good," he replied and walked into the sanctuary leaving Mike in the parking lot to complete the delivery project.

* * *

Bill Gaither's version of *He is Jehovah* resonated off the walls of the sanctuary as Randy walked in. "How does it sound with the new chairs, pastor?" Rick Kelly his music minister shouted over the booming volume from the sound booth.

Randy turned toward the booth and motioned for him to lower the volume then gave him a nod as it dropped. "Much better! We don't want to have any health insurance issues from members claiming they're going deaf!" he said with a tight smile, kidding.

"Hi, Pastor Randy!" he heard from behind.

Randy spun around to see Laurie accompanied by Stephanie Malone, the director in charge of their Open Arms homeless ministry. "Good morning ladies," he replied.

Laurie walked up to him as Stephanie moseyed off into her office. "Sean is a little late," she said as she rotated in place performing a quick survey then glanced at her wristwatch.

Randy looked to the rear lobby and saw a group of teenagers roaming around aimlessly. These were those who were in honor classes and were given staggered school hours. "He's obviously running late. He should be here soon," he said as he looked away from her to his music minister. Laurie blinked and nodded then walked off toward Stephanie's office. Her role as the assistant to Stephanie in the homeless ministry was strictly a voluntary position that brought her much spiritual fulfillment.

"We'll call you when we get all the chairs set up, pastor," Mike yelled out.

Randy saluted him then walked into his office to look out the windows for Sean's car. There was no sign of it. He grew pensive. He turned to make sure he closed his office door then pulled out his iPhone and pressed Sean's speed dial number. The rap music accompanying his greeting annoyed him. Seconds later: "Hi dad."

"Where are you, Sean?" Randy asked with a tinge of impatience. "We have a gang of youth waiting for you."

"Sorry I'm late. Just pulled into the driveway, dad," he said in contrition.

"You okay?"

"Fine, dad," he said. "Be right there."

Randy clicked off and shook his head, troubled.

* * *

TWO

The smell of burnt toast wafted through the house until it seemingly settled right outside Randy and Laurie's bedroom. Laurie sniffed the air several times before spraying on her perfume then went to her bedroom door. "Tiffy, you're going to set off the smoke alarm!" she shouted down the hallway.

"Not me," Tiffany yelled back. "It was Sean!"

Morning was a frenzied event at the Bradshaw house. Tiffany's first class at Broward College began at 8:30 A. M. with Sean's class at Florida Community College starting at 9:15 A.M. Randy made it a habit to be in his office by 8:30 A.M. with Laurie arriving sometime after 10 A.M. Collectively the bathrooms and kitchen were combat zones before breakfast.

With one hand on the refrigerator door, Laurie turned to Tiffany sitting at the kitchen table and said, "Sean on his way?"

Tiffany seesawed her head and replied, "I heard him in his room on his cell phone. I guess he'll be right down."

As Tiffany stood up Laurie took a hard look at her. She was all her at a younger age. Her red hair accentuated her radiant smile and brought out a warm luster on her slightly freckled face. As a twenty-three year old graduate student, her ideals and goals at one time were everything her parents wanted her to be. But now the outside world seemed to be having a great influence on her. In Laurie's mind the change was not necessarily good. "How's Alex doing in school?" her mother asked. Alex Sanders, the son of missionary parents to Italy was studying finance along with Biblical Studies giving him a double major. They were talking about marriage after he graduated while his parents talked about him pursuing Christian ministry.

"He's doing well," Tiffany replied with a nod. "He's sending out resumes to several brokerage firms both here in Florida and New York."

In the inner recesses of her heart, Laurie questioned with suspicion her daughter's choice of a man who spent many years growing up on the mission field and then in turn seemed to turn in a completely different career direction. No calling? "He's very smart so I'm sure he'll be scooped up right away," Laurie said, always looking to put a positive spin on things to begin the day.

"I'm not sure I want to marry him and relocate to New York at this point," Tiffany said as an afterthought, "but we'll see how things go." With that she reached on top of the refrigerator and brought down the box of donuts and pulled out a Boston cream and then stood at the counter eating it. Unusual. Normally she only had a cup of tea and a yogurt.

Laurie blinked. "Hungry this morning?"

"It's that time of the month," she replied with a smile then sat at the table to finish eating.

"Morning!" Randy said cheerfully as he entered the kitchen. He quickly surveyed the room. "Sean?"

"Finishing up, I guess," Tiffany allowed. Randy frequently looked to Tiffany as one who looked after her brother. He unwittingly seemed to ask her first as to his whereabouts.

Randy nodded in assent then smiled at Laurie. "I think I'll have scrambled eggs this morning, doll." His military background left him with the resolve where he needed three square meals per day in order to live right. To him the breakfast meal dictated one's strength for the remainder of the day.

"I read your mind," Laurie said while holding up two eggs in the air. "Dry rye toast?"

Randy nodded toward Laurie then turned to Tiffany. "Is Alex still talking to you about becoming a part of his church?" This was a sensitive subject between Randy and his daughter so he confined the discussion to the morning hours. Should a disagreement emerge, he preferred not to take it to bed with him. He valued his sleep.

Tiffany stuffed the remainder of the donut into her mouth then swallowed hard. "He knows all the college and career kids at Providence Church and really enjoys the friends he made there over the years. So he doesn't really want to change and come to our church," she said somewhat discordantly. "So…"she trailed off hesitantly.

Randy traded a look with Laurie. He was hoping there would have been a more spiritual verses societal reason given. "Does this mean that you'll wind up over there instead of at our church?" Randy ventured.

"I don't think so, dad," she answered with a curt shake of the head. "My family and roots are here."

"But Tiffy, if you marry him, that will change," Randy noted dryly.

"Um, I don't know about that," she replied after breathing deeply. "Too soon to tell. Right now I'm concentrating on getting through grad school."

Randy knew his daughter well. The conversation was over. He rubbed her hand and said, "We'll leave it there for today."

"I'm off," Tiffany announced and scooted out of the kitchen. Seconds later they heard the sound of her car keys rattling as she opened the front door. "See you at dinner!" she shouted.

Randy stared at the front door for a moment. Thoughts of his life with his daughter over the years gave him pause to reflect. There was a time not so long ago when she was so concerned with honoring the Lord and the church's homeless ministry that she fled their home to the streets because her mother would have no part in it. As time went on, God in his mercy brought Stephanie, a homeless renegade into their lives who would be God's vessel to bring Laurie to salvation. Yes, I remember, Lord, he thought. That was the happy ending to a serious family matter.

But as his children aged and entered into the mainstream of life and out from under the protective umbrella of sheltered youth and close family ties, their goals and purposes were changing rapidly toward what Randy called the wave of postmodernism. This threat to the corporate evangelical church looked to revamp the church, change the way Christians interact with their culture, and remodel the way we think about truth itself. Their version of truth itself is assumed to be inherently hazy, indistinct, and uncertain—perhaps even ultimately unknowable. This poison has radically permeated society where many Christians are unable to identify truth and form a biblical conviction that leads to living godly lives and becoming good citizens.

By choosing non-Christian colleges and associating with what Randy called the 'un-churched' his children were leaning more and more toward liberalism that he believed was in stark contrast to biblical teaching. In turn, this led to living the life that dishonors the God he and Laurie sought to serve. He did not preach isolationism. No one was asking them to become part of the monastic life living among monks who rarely travelled into public life and influenced only their peers. No, but his interpretation was that the professing Christian live a life that influenced others to desire Christ, and not the other way around where professing Christians were influenced to be more worldly.

"G'morning," Randy heard from behind as Sean sauntered in the room. He moved to the refrigerator and pulled out a bottle of vitamin water, snapping off the cap and began slugging it down. He was not much of a conversationalist in the morning.

Laurie shot him a look and shook her head and said with a chuckle as she brought Randy his eggs, "We use glasses in this house, Sean."

Sean drained the bottle then grinned. "No need to worry about backwash, mom." He shook the empty bottle. "There's nothing left," he added then tossed the bottle into their recycle bin.

"Some eggs with a corn muffin this morning?" Laurie ventured.

"No thanks, mom. I'll grab something at school," he replied.

"A little warm for long-sleeved shirts isn't it," Laurie asked as she looked at him in surprise. With Florida's tropical heat most residents wore short-sleeved shirts. Many wore sleeveless shirts. Few wore buttoned long sleeve shirts in the hot weather.

"My prof keeps the air down real low in class. I'm always cold," he replied.

"Tiffy said you were on your phone. Little early. Everything all right?" she asked. It was a mother's right to ask questions. This credo she believed was her mandated right for all the pain she suffered in childbirth.

If I brought them into the world, I have the right to know where they're going in this world, she maintained. Randy did not believe he had the right to be so intrusive, which was a point of contention at times.

"It was George," he replied. "Wants to get together after school."

Randy looked up from his eggs. He didn't care for George Mason. He only met him once and that one encounter unsettled him. He talked to him for only ten minutes but in that short time period he discovered George was a 'me-man.' All he talked about was himself and it occurred to him that his relationship with Sean was to only further his career or better his standing in life. He seemed very narcissistic. "Why don't you invite him to church this Sunday?" Randy ventured. This was Randy's way of keeping an eye on his son's friends while taking his spiritual temperature.

"I've invited him several times," Sean replied with a sigh. "But so far, no." Dismissively: "I'll keep trying." Seconds later: "Got to go folks."

Randy got the message: *Drop it.*

"Okay, Sean, we'll see you at church later today," Randy said, eyes narrowing on him as he stood in the doorway.

"Might be late, dad," Sean added. "Meeting with George for lunch at the bagel place after my last class."

"Oh, right," Randy remembered. "Okay, see you after lunch sometime."

"What days are you working this week?" his mother asked as he started to leave. Sean worked as a waiter at the Fisheries Restaurant in Plantation three nights per week to help pay for his tuition.

"Thursday, Friday, and Saturday," he answered on the fly.

The front door opened and door closed softly.

Laurie stood motionless looking at the front door from the kitchen then back at Randy. Her 'radar' as she called it went off in her heart. The keen sense of discernment the Holy Spirit gave her did not let too much pass unnoticed. "What's the matter?" she said, squinting at him.

Randy swallowed down the last piece of rye toast followed by several sips of his coffee. "Nothing," he said. Sometimes my children really disappoint me, he didn't say.

* * *

Sean felt his cell phone vibrate with a text message. He lifted it off his belt with one eye on his professor writing on the white board, the other on his phone. *Meet me at Santo's pizza after school luv tif.*

His leg started bouncing nervously. *Y whats up?* he texted.

Need 2 talk, Tiffany wrote.

Ok CU, Sean replied.

* * *

Tiffany sat in a window booth in Santo's Pizza scanning the parking lot for Sean's car. Where are you, my brother? She checked the time on her iPhone then shook her head before calling his number.

Connected!

"I'll be there in 5," Sean answered abruptly.

"Waiting!" Tiffany responded in kind then clicked off. Twenty minutes late was not cool in her mind. She walked to the counter and ordered a pie with two sodas.

Seventeen minutes later Sean walked in.

Tiffany gave him a disgruntled look then pointed to her wristwatch. "You said five minutes. You're late! Again!" she said with a scowl.

"Sorry, sis," Sean replied while sliding into the booth.

"I started without you," she said then pushed the second slice of pizza into her mouth. "It's getting cold," she added, "dig in."

Sean looked down at the pizza. "Not really hungry," he said with a shake of the head.

Tiffany dropped the rest of the pizza crust into the pan and gave him a hard look. Sean knew the look and started to nibble on his fingernails. "We're pretty tight aren't we, Sean?" she began with a piercing gaze. "I mean we can talk, right?"

Sean shrugged his shoulders. "Sure. What's up?" With that he hailed the waiter over and said, "I'll take a glass of vitamin water." He pushed away his soda as the waiter nodded and walked away.

"Well, I've been watching you carefully the last few weeks and you've been acting a little weird." She took a sip of her soda to seemingly gather her thoughts.

"Tell me straight," she snapped. "Are you *on* anything?" She looked around suspiciously. "I mean you're losing weight. Your eyes are red. You're cold all the time. You're late for almost everything. You stay in your room and bathroom for long periods. You don't have much of a social life at church or at school, with the exception of that weirdo you hang around with, George. You don't seem to have any interest in the young ladies at church either." Then she reached over the table and clutched his arm. "I'm your sister. I have your back. You can tell me, Sean."

A pause. For a millisecond Tiffany thought she saw a distress signal in his eyes.

"I'm fine," he replied then dropped his voice. "Don't worry about me, Tiff."

Tiffany squeezed his arm. "I do worry about you! You're my 'little' brother," she added in somber tones. Then she released his arm. "So—?"

Sean knew in his heart that his sister loved him. It was her that went for help when he was hit with a wild pitch of a lacrosse ball that nearly cost him his eye years ago. It was her that defended him at family feuds. It was her that encouraged him to stay close to the Lord while in college. It was her that ran interference between him and his parents. She was an important part of his life.

His stomach tightened as he contemplated his answer. Then he managed to appear unjustly accused, and slightly offended. Then suddenly: "I've been smoking a little weed. Nothing to get alarmed over."

Tiffany nodded. "That's what I thought. Well I–"

Sean quickly shifted his weight in the booth then abruptly stood up and looked over the table at her. "And what about you?" He placed one hand on his hip. "Are you pregnant? I mean you're putting on some pounds, girl."

I guess turnabout is fair play, she thought. She stiffened momentarily then: "If this were any other time I would tell you to mind your own business, but seeing how we're flushing things out," she said, fixing on him with a penetrating stare. "No, I'm not. It's just that I have my period. Satisfied?"

Sean bit his lip in silence as the waiter brought his vitamin water.

Both of them dismissed the pricking of their consciences by God's Spirit after they lied to one another.

* * *

THREE

Pastor Randy ascended the pulpit after his senior deacon, Lester Rogers, made the weekly church announcements then nodded to his music minister in recognition for his joyful worship service and said warmly, "Welcome to our Sunday Worship. We here at Plantation Church are truly blessed!" He pointed to the walls then to the new chairs and added, "Look around you. The Lord has enlarged our borders with this added building that was approved by our church membership and is now our new sanctuary. And we are delighted that every chair is occupied! We no longer have pews because we agreed to use the sanctuary as a place for fellowship and events such as weddings and social gatherings. We want to be able to use the sanctuary as a multi-purpose room to expand our facility to accommodate our neighborhood's growing needs. As good stewards of God's resources, our old building will serve as an annex for teaching purposes and a day care center in the near future." He pointed to Mike Rice who on cue bounced up several times in the new chair.

"Chairs are very comfortable, Pastor Randy!" Mike bellowed out.

Applause!

Randy quickly surveyed the congregation and noticed that not everybody applauded. "Now some of you may be thinking that we're going…" he paused and made quotations marks in the air and continued, "…too 'contemporary' or modern. Well let me assure you that we need to keep up with the times and that the days of the old pipe organ and pews are long since gone. In order for us to attract the unchurched we must stay relevant." He paused then pointed into the congregation at his board members and added, "This is the consensus of your board of trustees who together with the majority of the congregation believe along with myself that this is what is needed in order for our church to move forward." He nodded to Rick who sat on the sideline.

Rick stood up and walked to the pulpit as Randy walked off. "Please stand as we continue to worship!" he said jubilantly with open arms of praise. Rick had the excellent gift of exalting Christ in worship that in turn spiritually transported the congregation from the church to the very throne room of God. Many were so enraptured by his choice of hymns and his enthusiasm that they were enabled to forget their troubles and prepare their hearts to hear the word of God.

Moments later Randy returned to the pulpit as the congregation sat down. "Today we are finishing up our four-part series on 'Home Building.' Our sermon today will focus on God's view of sexual relationships." Several women snickered and many men grinned at the topic. "Okay, men, now that I have your attention," he continued with an expansive smile as several laughs echoed throughout the room, "be mindful that the Bible has much to say about sex.

"But I need to make a disclaimer first. I know there are young children present, and in view of what is happening in our culture where our youth are being indoctrinated in improper sexual behavior right in our elementary schools, we need to address this issues from God's perspective with them present. Hopefully this will produce wholesome dialog at home." He sorted through several pages of notes then explained: "Firstly, all sex outside of marriage between a man and a woman is condemned in the Bible. This is affirmed in both Testaments, found in Leviticus 18 and I Corinthians 6 and 7 among other places.

"Our God is a holy God! He is God and there is no other! His holiness is the standard by which we should live. Societal changes do not change the immutability of God—He is not capricious—he is the same yesterday, today and tomorrow. That is good news because His word tells us nothing can separate us from His love. Now many of us might have made some mistakes, some compromises, but He is ever ready and waiting for us to come to His throne in confession, seeking renewal.

"What does our Lord require of us? To know the Lord is to know His Word and His Word is very clear about marriage between a man and a woman. He made marriage sacred, something for young people to aspire to gain. As His children we are to be obedient to His decrees to keep ourselves pure in mind and body so we can worship and glorify Him.

"I as a pastor would be remiss if I did not address these subjects. The pulpit has a responsibility to teach the whole word of God." He paused to pull out a page from his notes. "Listen to this statement written in 1873 by evangelist/revivalist Charles G. Finney in his book, *The Decay of Conscience*: 'Brethren, our preaching will bear its legitimate fruits. If immorality prevails in the land, the fault is ours in a great degree. If there is a decay of conscience, the pulpit is responsible for it. If the church is degenerate and worldly, the pulpit is responsible for it. If the world loses its interest in religion, the pulpit is responsible for it. If Satan rules in our halls of legislation, the pulpit is responsible for it. If our politics become so corrupt that the very foundations of our government are ready to fall away, the pulpit is responsible for it. Let us not ignore this fact, my dear brethren; but let us lay it to heart, and be thoroughly awake to our responsibility in respect to the morals of this nation.' Mind you, this was penned in 1873 and baby, we've come a long way since then!

"The challenge from God," he continued, "is before us. If we as a member of the corporate church do not take responsibility for the decay of morals in this nation—" he waved his hands in the air, "then who is to blame? Can we honestly blame the unbelieving public or government for not legislating morality or should the church set the standard for society and in turn set the example for holy, Biblical living that ensures the well being of society?"

Silence.

He rested momentarily for the congregation to absorb his homily. He contemplated an altar call. No, this is not the right message for that, he thought. I don't want anyone to feel singled out as if they were guilty of some sexual sin that needed to be exposed—no I don't want to offend anyone. Then his eyes drifted toward the back of the sanctuary where a stranger walked aimlessly from one end of the lobby to the other. Uh-oh, Randy thought. Problem. He paused fractionally, scanned the congregation and spotting Stephanie, he motioned to her.

She recognized the signal and turned around to see the man in ragged clothes staggering through the lobby then peering into the sanctuary as if he were looking for a seat.

Stephanie stood up and quickly walked to the rear of the sanctuary to assist the ushers in what she thought could evolve into an incident. Moments later Laurie and Lester joined her. Their instincts and training dictated the unfolding of a potential problem.

Lester Rogers was the first responder who walked up to the man and placed his hand on the man's shoulder. "Welcome," he said with a smile. "Can we help you find a seat?"

"Maybe you would be more comfortable in this section over here," Laurie said pointing to a vacant area in an effort to divert him to where there were no members.

"I need to talk to the pastor!" the man said resignedly.

"Sure, we'll arrange that," Stephanie said while steering the man away to the secluded spot.

He tried to free himself from her hands. "I need to see the pastor!" he repeated an octave higher.

The commotion began to stir the congregation who started to turn around in their seats to see the disturbance. Randy took a deep breath while watching the unfolding drama in the rear of the church but managed to bring the worship service to a close without any invitation or recessional music.

"I NEED TO SPEAK TO THE PASTOR!" the man shouted as Randy descended the pulpit area. Lester nervously patted the man's back as he placed him in a seat while Laurie shook her head frantically looking for her husband to rescue them.

Stephanie glanced back into the sanctuary to see the congregation momentarily standing frozen in time then dispersing rapidly as Randy walked briskly toward her. She slowly stroked the man's hand for several minutes and then said calmly, "The pastor is right here. You're safe here so don't worry." Her soothing touch seemed to relax the man as he exhaled deeply.

"Yes, I want to be safe," he mumbled as his face contorted. "I want to be safe."

"I'm Pastor Randy. What is your name?" Randy could immediately see that he was indigent and needy.

"My name is Eddie Meegan and I just want to talk to you," the man choked out

"OK, let's talk as I'm sure these nice folks will excuse us."

* * *

It was still dark when his alarm went off at 6:30 A.M. Randy turned and looked out his bedroom window and noticed the Mockingbird on the sill. *A good omen*, he thought. Then the soothing song of the Mockingbird brought a smile to his face. "Good morning, Lord," he said aloud.

"Sleep all right?" he heard. He turned to see Laurie rubbing her eyes.

He sat up and said, "Okay, I guess. Little restless from yesterday, but overall pretty good."

Laurie pulled him back down into the bed. "Let's sleep in today," she said and began to rub his back. Randy smiled and turned to her. "You seemed so awfully tired yesterday when you got home," she said, "I was reluctant to ask you about the homeless man at the church. What happened? Why was he so afraid and upset?"

"His name was Eddie Meegan and he was afraid of God! I gave him the Gospel, told him he could have blessed assurance and prayed with him," Randy recounted.

"But what was his story? Was he afraid of dying?" Laurie asked.

"I don't know," Randy replied. "He kept saying he wanted forgiveness."

"Randy, did you try to get him some medical help or offer to get him a place where he could clean up and get some rest and be safe? I mean he was pretty ripe. I don't think he had bathed for weeks," Laurie noted.

"I asked him if he needed a place to stay and he said no," Randy responded.

Laurie became very agitated and got out of bed. This was not the man who was sure God wanted us to take part in the plight of the homeless, she thought. How many times had this man pontificated to me, *Whatever you do for the least of my brethren, you do unto me?*

"Randy there has been a shift in your thinking and behavior the last few months and I love you enough to tell you it is not to your credit. This whole building project and expansion program has distracted you from your first love, shepherding the flock."

"What do you want from me Laurie?" Randy asked.

"I want you to consider the divine appointment at our church yesterday. God sent a man searching for the truth and some comfort for whatever obviously had him so distressed and you obliged him by giving him the gospel and nothing else. He needed more," she explained in a lament. "If this had been a well-dressed man inquiring about his soul, would you have invited him home for a meal? Would you have asked how you could help him? Would you have provided hope and encouragement? I can't help but think that you had other things on your mind and brushed that poor man off."

She walked over and sat on the edge of their bed as a flood of thoughts cascaded into her mind. This was not the time for finger pointing or assessing blame when considering the sovereignty of God and how He is a God of detail, but when she looked at her husband she saw a man filled with regrets. "Can I get you something?"

He shook his head at first, then: "Dealing with the homeless is a difficult ministry and I know you are called to help the homeless but you're right, yesterday I was tired and wanted to get home. I have had so many things on my mind lately that I have even questioned the nature of my calling. After all these years, I'm wondering if I'm going in the right direction. I'm second guessing every decision," he added gloomily.

Laurie became very perplexed. Following your husband in church ministry is difficult enough when he knows where he's going. But when he's at a crossroads or on the edge of a cliff, that's quite another. "I'll put on a pot of coffee while you take a shower," she said. Randy nodded and walked into their bathroom.

*　*　*

Tiffany looked up from her second English muffin and coffee as Randy and Laurie walked into the kitchen. Physiognomy was one of her latent gifts. She read their faces immediately. "What's wrong, dad?"

"You know that homeless man that was making a commotion in the back of the church yesterday? Well, I prayed with him and explained the Gospel but then I just let him go without trying to meet any of his physical needs and I'm feeling guilty about it" Randy confessed.

"Oh, that's terrible!" Tiffany exclaimed. "Do you think he found a shelter as it was pouring rain last night?" She paused then added, "I'm sorry dad. I know this must be hard on you and mom."

Laurie poured Randy his coffee. "I'm not looking forward to questions from Stephanie about this man who sought out our church for safety" Randy said. "We all know that the procedure is to try to get as much information as possible so we can follow up and be of further help to the homeless person. If nothing else, they should leave our church knowing they are always welcome to return. The congregation will be curious as well."

Tiffany reached over the table and grabbed her father's hand. "Dad, stop beating yourself up, you gave him the Gospel and that's the most important thing," she soothed. The congregation will probably have forgotten it even happened by next week."

Laurie's gaze raked the both of them and then focused on Tiffany and asserted, "We always tell the truth no matter what complications the truth brings."

"Your right mom, just tell the truth about what happened and that you feel badly that you did not focus more intently on his physical needs as well as his spiritual needs. Like the Bible says, "'the truth will set you free'!"

"I just hope there is not a loss of confidence in me as the pastor," he said with eyes pleading for understanding. "The congregation would naturally think I would place him in one of our lodgings for the night to make sure he was out of the rain and safe from harm."

"So why didn't you take him to one of our safe shelters, dad?" Tiffany asked with a shrug of the shoulders.
Randy snuffled. "Not sure…" he trailed off then took another sip of his coffee

"Dad," Tiffany began as she placed her hand on his neck. "You know that I love you right?"

Oh, no! Here it comes! Randy took another slug of his coffee to brace himself for what he believed was coming: a tongue-lashing. "Of course."

"I may be in and out of the church since I'm in grad school," she intoned, "and as your daughter you may think I'm not qualified to comment, but I believe over the years that I've made an investment in your ministry. So you know I care. That entitles me to say what's on my heart. Right?"

Randy skewered her a look. "I guess—"

Laurie shook her head to warn her daughter not to go overboard, but Tiffany ignored the gesture. "I can see what's going on, dad. Ever since you started with the campaign to put up the new building with its huge mortgage payments, the direction of the church has changed."

Randy stiffened. "Now hold on, Tiffy—"

"Good morning family!" they heard from behind. They turned to see Sean leaning up against the kitchen doorway threshold. "What's happening?"

Tiffany turned and then scanned him from head to toe. Besides losing weight, he looked unkempt with mussed hair, a soiled shirt, and jeans with numerous holes. You look terrible!" she said with a warning frown. "You need a shower and a shave," she added in disgust.

His eyes flashed at the insult. He then gave her a lethal glance before he forced a smile. "Leave me alone, Tiffy! Why did you say that?"

Randy waved them off. "Okay you two," he said. "Let's be civil." He slowly rotated in his chair then said to Sean, "You need to go back to your bathroom and get cleaned up before you go to school."

Sean rolled his eyes then shrugged in his self-deprecating way, and left the room. "Whatever you say," they heard as he lumbered back to the bathroom.

Laurie and Tiffany were nodding, approving of Randy's command. "He's not taking care of himself," Laurie said as she held up a hand. "He needs a check-up."

Tiffany continued to stare at the vacated doorway, worrying about her brother. He does look terrible.

Randy shook his head slowly as a surge of anxiety came over him. My church and my family are in trouble.

He stood up and walked out of the kitchen, leaving both Laurie and Tiffany looking at each other in dismay.

* * *

Randy heard Laurie's footsteps as she followed him back to their bedroom. He walked into their bedroom bathroom and lingered several moments to gather his thoughts. "Lord, help," he whispered as several yawns came upon him. Yawns for him were not always from fatigue but often from anxiety. He kneaded his temples several times then mustered up the strength to handle any dispute then walked out. "We should talk," he said in an attempt to ward off any reprisals.

"Yes, we should," Laurie said as she paced the bedroom. "We need to think this through so we're on the same page."

Randy nodded then threw his hands up in the air then said somewhat apologetically, "I'm really upset about this and asking the Lord for direction."

Laurie read him too well. She lived with this man for over twenty-five years knowing full well his strengths and weaknesses. She knew when to encourage and when to exhort and when to admonish. She stopped pacing. "Direction!? Randy, do you want me to be honest?"

Randy nodded gloomily as the tension escalated. "Does it matter what I think?"

"Don't retreat into one-liners," she argued. "You're the pastor and must be prepared to answer any questions surrounding this incident." She escorted him over to their bed and pulled him down on the end. "Here's one of the issues you're going to face. It appears that you didn't want to be involved with this homeless man. We just put $2.5 million dollars into the new sanctuary. The thinking will be: we have plenty of money for a new building, but no money for this homeless man to receive the proper medical care that ended with him dying." She held his hand. "This can snowball into a big problem."

The realization of her report crashed in on him. He was on overload. He stared at her in helpless frustration. "I need to get to the office." With his head hung low he walked out and within seconds was on his way to the church.

Laurie shook her head as she recognized they hadn't prayed before starting their day.

* * *

FOUR

Randy recognized Mike Rice's car the moment he pulled into the church parking lot. He saw Lester Roger's car and two other deacon's cars as well. Moments later his music minister showed up. In his gut he knew giving the account of Eddie Meegan was going to be difficult but believed his staff was on his side and full of understanding.

"Good morning, Pastor Randy," Susan, his secretary said with a broad smile as he walked into the main office. Then she nodded and added, "Your staff is waiting for you in the library."

He forced a smile and replied, "Put on a pot of coffee for us, please."

Susan fretted not knowing what was going on. "Right away."

"Gather called Laurie this morning to find out how things were with the homeless man," Lester said as he walked into the room. "So I thought you would want to talk to us."

Randy marveled how quickly his staff assembled when a potential problem arose. He immediately sought allies and nodded in appreciation. "Yes, you're right. You saved me from making the phone calls."

"So what happened, pastor?" Mike Rice began, taking the roll as the spokesperson.

A muscle jerked in Randy's left cheek. "The man wanted to speak only to me. I gave him the Gospel and prayed with him. I tried to assuage his fears and then he left.

The men exchanged glances. "Was he going to a shelter as it had already started to rain when I left the church?" Mike Rice asked.

"I don't know," Randy replied.

Mike Rice shook his head and said glumly, "Was he on drugs or alcohol?"

"I don't know," Randy said. "I think so."

Randy mused momentarily then cracked his knuckles and said, "When we first saw the man he was ranting and raving. Insisting on talking to the pastor. Stephanie spoke to him first and she did not indicate substance abuse. Remember, she's had a lot of experience with the homeless and drug addicts. If she thought this man was a drug user, she would have said so."

"Okay, pastor," Mike said. "But it was obvious he needed some medical attention. As a church, we have worked very hard to provide alternatives to the street. Were any gestures made by you to secure a safe place for him to spend the night?"

"No," Randy replied. "And I don't know why."

Mike Rice raised his eyebrows while Lester Rogers simply grimaced then held up a hand. "I guess that's it," he said in torpid agreement and started to stand up.

"What do we tell the congregation?" Mike Rice asked. Lester Rogers sat back down again after shooting a look at Randy.

Randy realized he was not going to get away with a simple explanation as far as Mike Rice was concerned. But he was not going to be interrogated, especially not by his assistant pastor. "For one thing," Randy began with a defensive posture, "I need your support so as not to have any negative view on our church emerge. These things happen when you're dealing with the homeless. "So we'll just keep a low profile, and if anyone asks about the man, we'll tell them that he was given the gospel and that's all."

"No public announcement?" Mike asked, pulling back to look at him.

Randy shook his head and with a warning glance: "No need. No need."

Mike Rice got the message: Drop it. "You're the pastor," he said respectfully and stood up. The meeting was over.

"Coffee is ready," Susan announced at the doorway.

"I'll have mine to go," Mike Rice said with a smile as he lifted the container from the travel tray and walked out. The rest of the staff stayed several more minutes to enjoy their coffee, but Mike Rice's attitude troubled Randy.

Mike Rice walked into his office, closed the door, and went into prayer after setting his coffee on his desk. A thought jumped into his mind: Pastor certainly mentioned Stephanie frequently in his account of the homeless man. He took a slug of his coffee.

His spirit was unsettled. *Lord, are you planning to bring conflict into the ministry of Plantation Gate Christian Church?* He prayed he was prepared to handle it.

* * *

The beautiful sound of the piano and violin version of *Meditations from Thais* by Massenet filled Randy's office as he pondered the outworking of his staff meeting. He walked to the window and cast his eyes on the blue sky then to the horizon where dark altocumulus clouds were rapidly moving in. *Storm coming.*

He heard the office phone ring. Seconds later Susan announced: "Pastor Randy, Philip Van Fleming is on the phone."

Randy blinked then stiffened. Lord, let this be a good call. He walked to his desk then picked up the phone. "Phil, real good to hear from you!" he said brightly.

"Pastor Randy," he said in a booming voice, "thought I'd give you a holler! I would like to treat you to a round of golf down at the club—maybe next week if you're available."

Randy shot a short praise up to the Lord for one of His kisses that followed a rough 24 hours. "Sounds good!" Maintaining good relationships with his church members was vital to him.

"Outstanding!" he said. "I'll set it up and give you our tee time when I see you next Sunday."

"You're the best!"

Pause.

"Pastor Randy?" he ventured.

"Yes, Phil?"

"While I have your ear, I thought I'd just give my two cents on your sermon yesterday if you don't mind," he said, turning on his soothing voice.

"Not at all. Go ahead."

"Well Sandy and I were talking on the way home from Sunday service," he began, "and we both thought that maybe your homily was a little too 'heavy.' What we mean is that if there were visitors for the first time—and we believe there was—they might have been turned off by that sermon."

"You really think so?" Randy said in dismay.

"Well, yes. If we want to attract new people into our church, we need to give them what they need after a tough week of being kicked around by the world and their problems. You know what I mean," he argued. "As a church family we should be ministering to the sinner so they see our church as a place of rest and peace—not a place where they are made to feel uncomfortable. Making people uncomfortable at church is the death knell; they don't come back. This is not the way to build a church," he added didactically.

"Hmm," Randy emitted while growing pensive. "Something to think about."

"Then there's the church family," he continued. "Remember the expression, 'You're preaching to the choir'?" His voice dropped an octave. "Well, most of the veterans at Plantation have heard plenty of sermons on holiness over the years and are living as holy as they can," he asserted. "Both Sandy and I think there's a real need to deal with some family issues that bind husband and wife closer together. Shouldn't we concentrate on bringing parents and children to a better understanding of their relationship?" He paused to gather momentum then: "Randy, this business of bringing up issues on moral and societal change is okay coming from a upstart coming right out of a Baptist seminary, but for a qualified, experienced pastor like yourself, we think you should be focusing on…" he hesitated, "…what's that quote? Oh, yes, "'the pastor ought to have…one voice for gathering the sheep…' and that's what we need to do, gather the sheep, not scattering them by putting them on a guilt trip."

"So you're thinking I should tone the sermon down?" Randy asked.

"For what it's worth—my input—yes, I think you should. If only for a season, then you can compare the two approaches and see which one brings in the most fruit."

His argument and plan really made sense. Coming from Philip Van Fleming, a businessman who built a successful financial empire, his words had both weight and merit. "I look forward to having that golf game," Randy said.

"Thanks for listening, Pastor Randy," Philip said, and then clicked off, taking Randy's answer to be a 'yes.'

* * *

Randy hung up the phone then walked out of his office and through the connecting corridor into the sanctuary—the original sanctuary. Dating back to 1974, the 750-seat sanctuary boasted of an impressive brass spire, stained glass windows, and a fieldstone facade, set apart by a sprawling lawn augmented with prolific shrubbery that gave the church a cathedral-like appearance. Inside, the original church possessed traditional furnishing including oak pews, a wall-to-wall balcony once used as a choir loft, and 40 traditional light fixtures hanging from a 35-foot ceiling. The stage or altar featured a large oak pulpit in the center with a Baby-Grand piano to the left and a traditional pipe organ to the right.

Maybe we'll use this at Christmas, he thought as he stood and surveyed his old domain. I have fond memories attached to our original church. But this was for a different time, he mused. Organ has given way to the electronic keyboard. Piano has given way to the guitar and drums. This is what the people want. They no longer want the old conservative hymns and organ music. His heart beat faster. They no longer want the in-depth, convicting sermons or Bible studies. No—this is what they want. They want the breezy tour, which means no conflicting statements or arguments. Go light on doctrine. So who am I to kick against the bricks? He paused in his thoughts. *What do you want Lord?* he didn't say.

"Randy?" he heard. He turned to the back of the sanctuary to see Laurie approaching.

"Hi, babe," he said in a soft whisper.

"Pensive?" she asked walking up to him.

"No, just thinking," he chuckled.

Laurie held him by the hand and escorted him to the nearest pew and pulled him down on it. "Susan said the staff was waiting for you when you came in this morning. What did they want?"

Randy bit his lower lip. Confusing thoughts cascaded into his mind as Laurie's question could unfold in a manner not to his liking. "They wanted to know what happened with the homeless man. So I told them . . . " he trailed off.

"And—?

Randy inhaled deeply. "All but Mike Rice seemed to understand what happened. At times I don't think he really understands me."

Laurie squeezed his hand and smiled. "Do you mean at times he doesn't understand you or that at times he doesn't agree with you?"

Randy and Laurie were married over twenty-five years, and she knew him well. And he knew her well enough to know that she loved him but wouldn't let him get away with anything that seemed out of character for a pastor. "I guess you could say both," he eked out slowly. "He probably thought I should have fully explained every detail and nuance about the homeless man's needs."

You mean, Eddie Meegan? Laurie noticed his impersonal touch. "What about the rest of the staff?"

"Seemed okay with my explanation," he replied with a shrug.

Laurie shot a prayer up to God. *Lord, only you can reveal truth.* "Well, if there are any repercussions," she said in her soothing voice, "then we'll deal with them as they come up."

Randy nodded in relief.

"What did Philip Van Fleming want?"

I need to talk to Susan about being a blabbermouth. Randy wrinkled his nose. "He called to invite me to play golf with him next week."

Laurie's antennae telescoped. "What was the price tag?"

Randy shook his head. "Oh, nothing. He just wanted to comment on my sermon, that's all."

Laurie let his hand go. "Wilson Randolph Bradshaw," she said with clear precision. "I know the nature of the beast, and he doesn't just call to throw bouquets around. What did he want?"

He hated it when she called him by his birth name. It meant escalation. "He thinks my sermons should be less intrusive and more—"

"More 'people friendly,'" she completed his sentence.

"Well, I guess—" he fumbled as his guts began to wretch.

"So that's it," she summarized gruffly. "He thinks his money has sway in our church and that he can throw it around as he sees fit in order to dictate policy."

Randy swallowed hard. "I believe he has our church's best interest at heart, doll," he replied with pleading eyes.

"Well I don't," she replied. "I believe he is the voice of the modern movement in the church that spells 'compromise' in order to fill the buildings."

"You really think so?" he asked.

Laurie saw weakness. No, not weakness it was more like indecision. She was troubled. "Randy, the corporate church is no longer about the good news of the gospel of the Lord Jesus Christ and all He has done, it has become about 'finding peace within yourself' and 'embracing the new you.' That's what Van Fleming is talking about. It's a colossal shift and concession from what we are called to preach."

"You really think so?" he repeated.

"Yes, I do!" she said emphatically. She stood up. "Why don't you go talk to Mike and see what he has to say about your phone call from Van Fleming?" She looked up at the ceiling lights, then to the organ and piano. Finally she gave the pews a hard stare before a wave of spiritual nostalgia swept over her. "Maybe we need to get back to the days when we did church the old fashion way. Worshipping God instead of trying to please people."

After biting his lower lip again he replied, "Yes, I will talk to him."

They walked out of the original sanctuary together. As they walked Randy suddenly placed Philip's quote, only the corrected version by John Calvin: "The pastor ought to have two voices: one, for gathering the sheep; and another, for warding off and driving away wolves and thieves. The Scripture supplies him with the means of doing both." Lord, don't let a spirit of confusion overpower me.

* * *

Randy stood in front of Mike Rice's office door with two cups of coffee. He always believed an unexpected complementary cup of coffee in a hostile environment acted as a peace offering. This time he also brought two Boston cream donuts as an added incentive to bridge any gap between them.

He knocked softly at the door. "Mike, it's Randy," he said. "Can we talk?"

"Come in, pastor," he heard through the door.

Randy walked in to see Mike reading his Bible at this desk. He glanced down to see he had turned to 2 Timothy chapter Four, and quickly recognized the passage as the instructions the apostle Paul gave to Timothy regarding the call to protect sound doctrine. A quick read of his face told Randy that Mike was perplexed. "Mike," he began as he placed the offering on his desk then sat down, "I sensed our staff meeting left you slightly out of sorts, so I wanted to hear from you individually if there is a problem."

Mike nodded curtly. "Pastor, I have always defended your decisions," he began after sipping his coffee, "and you know that I've not always agreed with them, but for the sake of unity, I supported you. But lately I've noticed a departure from our mission statement and philosophy of ministry and today you're telling of the way you handled the homeless man, Eddie Meegan has left me disturbed."

Randy respected Mike and Suzy's dedication to Plantation Gate Church, and believed that he could count on him to represent himself and his pastor in such a fashion as to give a good report to any inquiry, but now he thought he had lost sight of the church's vision. "Okay, I can respect your view, Mike," he explained, "but then again, I must take precautions to protect the future of our church ministry from any unfavorable publicity. This means that after five years, Plantation Gate has lost some serious people who at one time were solid members, and I've taken a close look at this and believe much of our attrition rate is because of the homeless ministry. So in view of this I am looking to move in another direction. This had a direct bearing on my decision and announcement."

Mike tapped his fingers sequentially on his desk as he pondered his response. Seconds later: "I'm afraid we might be going in the wrong direction, that's all," he replied cautiously. "The both of us are looking for God's blessings on this ministry and I personally am afraid of adopting the philosophy of ministry that caters to the man in the pew and not to the Spirit of God." He stood up. "If that happens—"he paused and his breath caught in his throat then added, "I'm out of here!"

"Mike, you know that I love you and Suzy and enjoy working with you here at Plantation Gate," he entreated softly. "You both are an important part of this church and I want you to know that I would never implement any policy that would endanger this ministry, nor would I look to modify our vision without running it through our staff and trustees." He stood up and began to fill with tears. "You need to trust me and get behind me."

Mike suddenly became swept up in the emotionalism. "Okay, pastor," he said. When it came to these issues, he had to trust the Lord to bring about the resolution. He could not remain in a state of conflict.

Randy walked to him and put his arms around him then gave him a brotherly kiss on the cheek. "Thanks, Mike. I knew I could count on you."

Are we trusting in the Lord, or are we trusting in Randy? Mike thought as Randy walked out of the room.

The thought of a storm coming flew out of Randy's mind.

* * *

FIVE

Randy slowly raised one eyelid to peek at the clock on the bedroom end table then rolled over to his other side and pulled the covers over his shoulders. "Yesterday was a killer day, Lord," he whispered. "Today has to be better." He snuggled down in their king sized bed for another five minutes before reaching over to wake Laurie. *Where are you, babe?*

"Time to rock and roll, Mr. Bradshaw," Laurie announced as she walked into their bedroom.

He sat up in the bed and smiled luminously. "You're dressed already?" Normally he was the early riser who put on the coffee.

"Having breakfast with Suzi this morning," she replied sparkly.

Randy rubbed his eyes. "Oh, right. I forgot."

"You might want to drop in on your son and get him up for school. I knocked on his door a few times but there was no answer."

"Late night studying, no doubt," he replied. *I hope that's it,* he didn't say. "Will do."

"Tiffy is just getting up and will have breakfast with you guys. I'll see you later down at the church." She threw him a kiss as she slipped her handbag over her shoulder. "Love you."

"Love you more!" he replied and lifted himself out of the bed and walked into the bathroom and looked into the mirror. "Getting old, pal," he said aloud. *Age is a matter of spirit,* he reminded himself. The image of him sporting a mustache in his Navy days popped into his head. He ran his fingers through his hair. His hairline was receding, but no bald spots. *No gray hairs yet, maybe I'll grow another mustache to look younger.* He looked at the horizontal lines on his forehead and then the laugh lines on his face and then he felt the start of some bulging around his eyes. *Hmm. Something to think about.*

* * *

Randy heard Tiffany taking her shower as he knocked three times on Sean's bedroom door then stopped and listened.

No response. *Music?*

He turned his head toward the door to hear the sound of rock music at low volume. He wasn't familiar with the tune but assumed it was coming from one of Sean's many electronic devices. He knocked again, this time more forcefully.

No response *again.*

He slowly opened the door to see Sean lying in his bed with his shirt on. He walked to his bed and noticed Sean's iPhone sitting on his pillow next to his head. He glanced down at the iPhone and read the title as the song played on: *Lady Gaga at Miami. What the—?* "Sean, time to wake up," he said, modulating his voice carefully. "You don't want to be late for class."

Sean remained inert. Randy tugged on his pillow and raised his voice. "Sean, you need to get up!"

"Is he okay?" Tiffany asked from the doorway.

Randy turned to see her standing in her robe toweling her hair. "I guess," he said and then shook

Sean's shoulder. "Sean!" he said, his voice vibrating with intensity.

Sean squirmed in his bed and then buried his head under his pillow. Randy sighed in relief then shook Sean's shoulder again. "Time to get up."

Sean turned and faced his father. "What time is it?"

"It's time to get up," Randy repeated impatiently then hit the *Pause* button on Sean's iPhone music application. *What in the world possessed you to download that hideous album?*

Sean bolted upright. "Okay, dad, no problem," he said half-apologetically.

Randy turned to Tiffany and gave her a sidelong look she couldn't decipher. Then he walked out of the Sean's bedroom as Tiffany shook her head in disgust. *We need to talk, bro.*

* * *

Randy stood in the kitchen sipping his coffee as Tiffany sat at the table finishing off an English muffin and jelly. Silence permeated the room as Tiffany tried to read the scene. She knew her father well and recognized his escalating anxiety level as he waited for her brother to show up. *He must be contemplating his next move.* "Can I get you something to eat, dad?"

"No thanks, honey," he replied.

Tiffany noticed her father was grinding his teeth. "You sure?"

"Not hungry," he said tiredly.

Tiffany watched the kitchen clock as she finished her breakfast recognizing her father's restlessness increasing with every passing moment. Instinctively she knew she couldn't leave the room until Sean appeared, if only to mitigate an argument.

Randy exchanged glances with Tiffany for fifteen minutes until finally: "I'm going to his room and get him," he said in helpless frustration.

Tiffany pointed down the hallway. "Here he comes, dad," she said in relief.

Sean ambled into the kitchen wearing jeans and a lightweight parka and waved to his sister. "G'morning," he said then looked at his father and added, "Sorry about this morning, dad. Studied into the wee hours of the morning."

Randy shot a look at Tiffany then snuffled. "You're going to tell me that we could barely wake you because you were exhausted from studying? Now that's a reach, Sean, and you know it!" Randy looked to Tiffany for support, but her face said: *I'm neutral.* "Explain to me what happened last night," Randy continued, his voice conveying disbelief.

Sean moved to the refrigerator and removed an energy drink, snapped off the cap and took a slug before answering. "Dad, honest, it's exam week at school and I'm cramming. I spent several hours studying over at Cindy's house, then I came home late and worked on the books until"—he hesitated to check the clock—"probably three in the morning."

Randy blinked at his reply then looked at Tiffany to see her give Sean a warning glance. "This *is* exam week, dad," she said in his defense. No longer neutral.

Randy deflated. He suddenly felt his heart rate slowing. *Don't jump to conclusions*, he commanded himself. *Sounds reasonable.* "Cindy Allen?" he asked, changing tracks. "The girl I met at our church some weeks ago?"

Sean nodded. "Yes. Her father works for Florida Power and Light. Nice family," he explained.

Randy vaguely remembered the name. They had visited Plantation Gate's worship service one Sunday. He couldn't place Cindy's face, but recalled noticing the name *Allen* written on an offering envelope. They appeared to be an upstanding family. *Let it go*, he ordered himself. *Once I begin to doubt my son, we're in trouble.* "Okay, let's drop it," he finalized. He walked to the counter and grabbed a banana from the fruit basket and then turned to Sean. "See you at church later this afternoon for youth." Then he smiled at Tiffany, "Have a blessed day." Minutes later he was out the front door.

* * *

Tiffany mechanically placed her dishes in the dishwasher while listening for their father to drive away. *We're safe.* She looked at her brother wearing a muted smirk then turned to him in fury and yelled, "You pulled it off, you little liar!"

"Leave me alone, Tiffy!" he screamed in her face.

Tiffany slammed the door of the dishwasher then jumped to his side and pulled up one sleeve of his parka. "Now let's see what's really going on!" she demanded.

He jerked his arm back but not before she saw multiple red sores on his forearm. "Now I know why you've been wearing long sleeve shirts and parkas!" she snapped. "You're on drugs!" She fell back into her chair. "What are you taking?" She pointed to him and snarled, "Those are track marks. Are you on heroin? Oxycodone?" She filled up with tears. "Sean, I'm you sister, you can tell me. I want to help you," she pleaded.

He glanced at her, but he remained utterly still, a statue. Only his eyes moved. Then: "Tiffy, I've been under a doctor's care for impotency and he gave me testosterone shots to take. That's what I'm on."

Her whole countenance changed. Her eyes flashed several times. The revelation stunned her, disarming her completely. She clapped her hand over her mouth momentarily. "Impotency?"

"Yeah, I know girls don't know much about it," he said with raised eyebrows, "but it's not the kind of thing you go around broadcasting. It sort of keeps me concentrating on ministry and school, not on girls . . . " he paused, "…for now, anyway."

"Do dad and mom know?"

"Like I said, it's not the thing you talk about over lunch. I'll get around to bringing dad and mom into the circle soon."

Tiffany smiled. "Well I feel one-thousand percent better now," she said expelling a long theatrical sigh.

Sean reached over and pulled his sister to himself. "I love you, Tiffy. Thanks for watching my back."

"Always," she said, drying her eyes.

* * *

Tiffany stood looking out the Broward College library window watching the raindrops cascade down the glass as if they were tears on her face. She grew sad. Doubts crept into her heart as if they were some kind of virus that waited to manifest itself. Instinctively she realized that to ignore that doubt would bring greater harm. Her spirit troubled her until the thought came into her mind that what her brother had told her seemed to be the cause of her misgivings. *No, I cannot allow suspicions about my brother to take root. But if something is wrong inside him...*

She cast her reservations aside and walked to the library computer where she went Online to a search engine and keyed the word *testosterone* in the query box. Her eyes were riveted to the monitor as she scrolled down page after page, copying, pasting, and highlighting until she had over four pages of selected notes printed. From there she meandered over to a lounge chair to study her notes. The research troubled her. The highlighted portions stated that anabolic steroids, technically known as anabolic-androgenic steroids (AAS) or colloquially as "steroids," are drugs that mimic the effects of testosterone in the body. They increase protein synthesis within cells, which results in the buildup of cellular tissues, especially in muscles. In medicine testosterone is used to stimulate bone growth and appetite, induce male puberty, and can contribute to increases in body weight as well as accelerate hair growth. As early as 1937 injections of testosterone propionate was reported to have been given to German soldiers in the form of anabolic steroids during the Second World War with the aim being to increase aggression and stamina, citing Adolf Hitler, himself, according to his physician, was injected with testosterone derivatives to treat various ailments. She paused: *Sean has not gained an ounce in the past two months; in fact he's losing weight. There has been no muscle growth that I've observed. Nor have I seen any significant difference in his hair or beard.*

She read on: "Testosterone injections are typically administered into the muscle, not into the vein, to avoid sudden changes in the amount of the drug in the bloodstream, and because estered (combined compound) testosterone is dissolved in oil, intravenous injection has the potential to cause a dangerous embolism in the bloodstream." She shook her head. "This can't be," she whispered to herself. "Something is not right here. I'm being lied to. He's injecting into his arms."

She highlighted the section that recommended testosterone-containing creams and gels that are applied daily to the skin were available. *Why not use them? And why not go to a doctor and get Viagra to help with your impotence?*

The last page contained warnings that alarmed her. She read that anabolic steroids can cause many adverse effects including the damaging of the immune system and harmful changes in cholesterol levels and can increase the risk of cardiovascular disease. Testicular atrophy from the suppression of natural testosterone levels, which inhibits production of sperm, has also been reported. Acne is fairly common among anabolic steroids users due to stimulation of the sebaceous glands by increase testosterone levels. *Sean has no acne.* Then she focused on: "Testosterone injections appear to act through the mesolimbic dopamine system, a common substrate for drugs of abuse." She stopped reading abruptly, rolled up the four pages and put them in her backpack. *Bro, we really need to talk.*

* * *

Crossing his legs did nothing to stop the uncontrollable reflex of what he believed was RLS as he sat taking the statistics exam. His left leg twitched unexpectedly along with his foot shaking noticeable until he consciously focused on the dilemma. He took his eyes off the exam booklet then bit his lip to redirect his attention. The shaking stopped. Then he reached down into his pant pocket to feel the plastic baggie and the caplets it contained. *Not now*, he told himself. *I have to get through this exam.*

He closed his eyes momentarily. Euphoric thoughts lingered. He zoned out and suddenly saw that he was sunning himself on a blanket at the Fort Lauderdale beach. *Ahh! Yes!* He transported himself to the Breakers in Boca Raton and saw himself sitting at the bar having a few stiff drinks with some lady he did not recognize.

A tap on the shoulder!

"Sean, you need to work on this test," he heard.

He jerked his head as he snapped out of the daydream. "Right, prof," he said apologetically. He took his hand out of his pocket then scratched his head in a vain effort to remember the formulas in cumulative percentages and percentile equivalents he attempted to memorize. It wasn't working.

Fifteen minutes later he stood up and walked to his professor, handing him the incomplete exam while giving him an *I did the best I could look.*

* * *

Sean could feel the sweat running down his chest as he walked to his car. He lifted his parka at waist level and fanned himself as he walked. Once in his car he looked into the rearview mirror. Oh—" he used a vile word—"I hope my prof didn't see this." His eyes were watering along with a runny nose. Internally he felt nauseas. He reached over to his console and lifted out a bottle of water then pulled the baggie from his pocket, removing two of the white caplets, and then swallowed them with a huge gulp. He sat with the windows open for ten minutes then headed for the church to meet with the youth.

* * *

Minutes after he arrived, Randy walked to the church's kitchen as the aroma of freshly made soup guided him. The strong smell of chicken soup filled the air in the state-of-the-art kitchen adjoining the fellowship hall then circulated through the air conditioning system, alerting the staff that today was soup kitchen day for the homeless. The fellowship hall could easily accommodate over one hundred and fifty patrons at one time.

"Come to help out?" Stephanie asked Randy as he walked into the kitchen to see her holding a ladle and stirring a large pot. Then she pulled out the ladle to sip a small portion then said, "Want to taste?"

Randy nodded as he noticed how nice she looked in her designer jeans and heals with an apron on top of a blouse that seemed to cling to her body. He caught sight of Laurie setting up tables in the fellowship hall and said, "Sure." Then he walked over to Stephanie and then paused to move several strands of her hair away from her eyes. Then he sipped from the spoon as she held it to his lips. "Outstanding," he said. Stephanie blinked several times as Laurie walked in, then turned away from Randy and continued to tend to the soup.

"Mike is running late," Laurie announced as she approached Randy, "so I'm setting up the lunch room."

"You're the wo-maan," he said sarcastically.

Laurie held up her arms and flexed her muscles. "The right man for the job is a wo-maan," she teased. They all laughed. Seconds later Laurie looked at Randy and gestured to follow her out of the kitchen.

"What's up, babe?" he said as she walked him to a far corner of the fellowship hall.

"I didn't want to get into it last night or this morning, but how did things go with Mike yesterday?" she asked. In ministry life, husband and wife sometimes take the night off and don't discuss potentially inflammable subjects until the following day. This enables the family to remain civil.

"Fine, I guess."

Laurie probed deeper. "The 'I guess,' tells me otherwise. What did he say?"

"He didn't approve of the way the homeless man was treated."

"What else?"

Randy gulped in a mouthful of air. "He thinks the ministry at Plantation is going in the wrong direction."

Laurie nodded curtly. "I had breakfast with Suzi," she replied, "and she thinks the same way."

Randy bit his lip reminding himself that Laurie and Suzi were tight. "What did she say?"

"They both agree they will give you full support provided you don't cave in to the current movements that are harming the corporate church, namely all the 'isms.'"

Randy snorted. He knew Mike's view on the 'isms' that included post-modernism, secularism, materialism, hedonism, narcissism, existentialism, and on and on until his complaint stuck in his throat. "I know how he feels about the 'isms' and I have assured him in the past that we will not go down that path," he replied in defense.

"Well, they believe that when you pander to those who are big tithers that you are sliding down the slippery slope into the 'isms." She stopped and pointed to the kitchen. "Eventually they see the church's philosophy changing that will ultimately eliminate the homeless ministry to which they are 110 percent involved. They heard of the way you treated Eddie Meegan and that gave them more ammunition for their cause."

"Look, Laurie," he said as he blinked in listless agreement, "I told Mike that I will never implement any policy that would endanger this ministry and that he—" he paused to put his arm around her, "—and the rest of my people, need to trust me as their pastor to do the right thing to protect the future of our church."

Lord, this man knows all about your deeds, but you need to show him your ways. "Okay, Mr. Bradshaw, you're the pastor," she replied with a smile and started to walk back to the kitchen then stopped abruptly and turned. "What about Sean? Did he get off to school okay?"

Randy gave her thumbs up. "All is well," he said then walked to his office.

"Is everything all right with you two?" Stephanie asked the very second Laurie walked in.

"We're fine," Laurie answered.

Really?

* * *

Freddy Lucas stood at the rear door of the new building looking into the parking lot then rushed back into the youth room and announced to the others in his group, "Hey, guys, Sean is circling the cars in the lot as if they were covered wagons!" He snickered then added, "You need to come and see this." Four of the youth dropped their Ping-Pong paddles and followed Freddy to the door facing the parking lot.

"What the—?" one of the youth exclaimed. "What's he doing?"

"He's circling the cars," another said. "Maybe he thinks he's the wagon train master."

After five revolutions, Freddy turned to the group and said, "I'm going to get the pastor. Something is wrong."

"No!" the other four in the group insisted. "Let it be," the spokesperson said. "We don't want to get him in trouble."

Freddy nodded.

Moments later Lester walked over and joined them at the door. He quickly assessed the situation and then turned to Freddy. "You folks return to your youth room. I'll take care of this."
Freddy nodded respectfully and waved them back to the youth room as Lester walked off to Randy's office.

The pastor's door was wide open as Lester approached. He knocked on the doorjamb and said nervously as he looked at Randy standing by his bookshelves, "Pastor, you need to come with me right away! Something is going on with Sean."

Randy whirled instinctively as his mind seized up in panic. For Lester to be alarmed, it had to be serious. He motioned to Lester to refrain from advising Susan then said torpidly as he followed in near lock step behind him, "What's happening?"

"Your boy is acting very peculiar. He's circling the parking lot in his car," he explained as they rushed along. "Freddy Lucas spotted him and when I came in, I sent them back to the youth room."

"Good call."

From the door Randy saw Sean's car stopped at the far corner of the parking lot. He shot praise up to God then said to Lester, "I'm going out to him. You stay here and watch the door."

"Right, pastor," Lester agreed. Lester was the consummate loyal servant of the church and to his pastor. To him, whatever was going on with the pastor and his son was a private matter. If the pastor wanted him to know, he would tell him. From his sentry position he would deflect any inquiries. In his heart, Lester believed at this juncture it included Laurie and Stephanie.

As Randy neared the car he heard the engine racing. His eyes immediately spotted Sean slumped sideways in the driver's seat. He quickly opened the driver's side door as Sean's body sagged and nearly fell out of the vehicle. Randy grabbed him then pulled Sean's foot off the accelerator then reached over and turned off the ignition.

Seconds later Sean began to rally out of his stupor speaking incoherently. Randy pulled him out of the vehicle and slammed him against the side of the car. He then noticed two empty beer cans on the passenger's seat.

He shook Sean's shoulders and yelled in his face, "Sean! What are you doing!?"

Sean belched several times then said, "Oh, hi, dad. I came right from school."

"Sean, you're drunk!" Randy exploded. "You're a disgrace to our family and to this church!"

No response.

Randy mouthed an expletive then closed the car door and then put his arm under Sean's shoulder and slowly walked him around the car several times before walking him toward the rear door of the building. Once there, Lester assessed the scene and held the door open for them. "Should we bring him to your office?"

"No," Randy said. "Let's get him to the men's room as discreetly as possible." Lester nodded then darted ahead to watch and clear other persons.

Randy carried Sean to the restroom vanity, turned on the faucet then splashed cold water in his face. "Whoa!" Sean said roughly, pulling back. "What's going on?"

"Sean! Come out of it!" Randy snapped in his face. Sean's head lolled to one side as Randy propped him up against the vanity counter. Within seconds Sean began to teeter.

Lester saw Randy's face. He had to officiate. "Sean," Lester said as he held Sean's arms, "you have to meet with the youth group! They need you." *Uh-oh, what's this?* Lester had inadvertently pulled up Sean's parka sleeve and took a hard look at his arms. *Not good.* Lester hesitated, reassessed, and responded. "Pastor, I think Sean should go home."

Randy turned his head to hear voices outside the restroom. It was Laurie and Stephanie walking by. "I agree. We need to get him home," Randy replied just above a whisper.

Lester handed off Sean to his father then offered: "I'll take him home in my car and then sometime later today we can drive his car to your house."

"Good plan," Randy said with a shake of his head. *This is a continuing nightmare.* Lester peeked outside the restroom door then left unnoticed to get his car.

As Randy held his son in his arms his mind wandered. *How did we get here, Sean? What is missing in our family, in your life? Isn't Jesus enough?*

"Dad," Sean said as he rallied. "I'm really sorry about this!" His volume heightened. "My exam was a bear!" Slurring: "I'm real—ly sor—ry about this!"

"Shush!" Randy replied, patting his back. "Let's get you home."

The restroom door swung open. "Coast is clear, pastor. Car's outside," Lester announced in hushed tones.

They marched Sean outside and put him in Lester's car. "The key to the house is under the planter at the side door. Put him in bed. I'll get home as soon as I can."

"Will do, pastor." Moment's later Lester drove out of the parking lot to Randy's home with Sean lying across the back seat. Fast asleep.

* * *

"Two phone calls for you, pastor," Susan said as he came into the church office. "One from Philip Van Fleming, the other from Lester."

"Thanks, Susan," he said, looking at the floor as he walked.

"Everything all right?" she asked. Susan had a self-imposed ministry to look after her pastor's welfare. If he were downcast for any reason she believed it her duty to encourage him.

Randy forced a smile. "I'm fine." He closed his door behind him then called Lester on his cell phone. Three seconds later Lester read the church number on his Caller ID. "Lester, pastor Randy. How's my boy?"

"Sean is safe at home," Lester replied. "I put him in his bed then locked up the house. I'm on way back to the church now."

"Come to my office when you return." He clicked off.

His office door swung open!

Randy turned in automatic alarm to see Laurie standing with the doorknob in her hand and Stephanie looking over her shoulder. "Where's Sean? His car is in the parking lot but he's not in the church."

Think fast! Randy commanded himself. "He must have come down with the flu or something because he came to the church—acting sickly—so I had Lester drive him home."

"Oh, that's a relief," Laurie replied. "I thought something terrible had happened."

"He'll be fine, don't worry." Afterthought: "I suppose we should have all gotten the flu shots." Randy shot a look at Stephanie as she rolled her eyes.

"Okay, love," Laurie said. "We'll be in the kitchen getting ready for the luncheon."

Randy gave them a dismissive wave as they departed and then picked up his desk phone. *Do I really want to talk to Philip now? No.* He hung up the phone. *Later.* He walked to the window to see Lester pulling into the parking lot. *Good.*

What seemed like a long duration was only several minutes before Lester walked into his office, closing the door behind him. "Pastor," Lester began, "you're son has a problem. I think you should talk to him and find out what it is."

Randy's brow furrowed. "I've talked to him about his drinking before, but it's something that he struggles with and I'm at a loss, frankly."

Lester stared at the floor, hands in his pockets. Randy blinked rapidly, and looked away. Lester shook his head. *No way in hell am I butting in to this family secret.* "Well what I think you need to do is to *really* talk to him. Find out what's going on in his head. Remember, you're not only his dad, but you're his pastor as well."

This man is your confidant, Randy reminded himself. *You can talk to him. He has been a loyal servant throughout the years. You can talk to him.* "We've drifted apart over the past few years, I'm not sure I can connect with him anymore," he confessed sorrowfully. "I mean since he's been going to college there seems to be a gap in our relationship."

"That happens to most of us when our kids leave the house and start out on their own," Lester advised. "But the answer is always *communication.* You need to communicate with him."

"Yes, I know historically that's what happens, but when it happens in your own house, it's somehow different," he argued. "We don't have to worry about our Tiffany. I can communicate with her. And I know she's really a good girl. We know she's behaving herself. But with Sean—" he paused and sighed deeply—"things are different. He's like a wild card in our deck of cards."

"Can you appeal to him in the Spirit?" Lester ventured. "Tell him that what he's doing is wrong?"

Randy shrugged his shoulders. "Maybe, not sure. I know he's involved here at our church, but I'm not sure about his relationship with Christ." His stomach flipped. "Just because he's involved here doesn't mean he belongs to Jesus."

Lester pondered his pastor's words. If he knew the answer to that he would rival Solomon. "Hmm, yes. Well, if you want my advice I just think you should sit down with him and ask him about his testimony and how it is affecting others. Maybe that will lead you into uncharted waters and he will open up to you."

A droplet formed in Randy's eye. He walked over to Lester and put his arm around him. "I'll try, and thanks for being my friend as well as a loyal servant here at Plantation Gate."

Lester hugged his pastor. "Let's get Sean's car home."

* * *

The moment Tiffany opened the front door of her home she knew she wasn't alone. She could hear the faint sound of music coming from Sean's room. She glanced at her wristwatch then spotted Sean's backpack on the vestibule floor. "Sean!" she yelled. "Hey, what's up?" *Nothing.*

She walked to his bedroom and slowly opened the door. He was sleeping with his iPhone on his pillow with the rest of his body under the covers. Tiffany noticed his pants and parka were strewn on the floor and realized that he undoubtedly woke up, undressed, and then fell back into bed. She paused momentarily then surreptitiously walked into the room and picked up his pants. She rummaged through his pockets and pulled out the plastic baggie then took out one of the white caplets and stuffed it in her pocket, then swiftly replaced the bag in his pants before turning off his iPhone music.

"Time to wake up, bro," she said while tugging on his pillow. Sean moaned then tossed and turned several times. She raised her voice. "Time to wake up, Sean!"

His eyes fluttered. "Hi, sis," he said, partially lucid. How he got into the bed had not occurred to him at this point.

"Thought we'd have a little chat," she replied. She reached into her backpack and pulled out her library report and then threw the papers at him. "You have lied to me," she began. "I did research on testosterone, and you're not on that!" She pointed to the papers and added, "Time to come clean, bro. What is really going on?"

Sean pulled the covers up to his neck. "Okay, okay, so I told you a little fib. No big deal," he replied with a grin.

"And—?"

"The truth is that—" he paused—"No! I'm not going to say anything unless you promise me that you won't tell mom or dad."

"Maybe yes, maybe no!" she shouted. "At this point you have little bargaining power!"

"Okay, okay," he said as his lips twitched. "The truth is that I did start out taking testosterone shots in the butt, then as time went on and things got crazy out there–

–" he paused again and bit his lower lip—"I migrated to cocaine."

Tiffany filled up with tears. "SEAN, LOOK AT YOURSELF!" she screamed in his face. She reached over and pulled the covers away to expose his arms. "Just look at what you're doing to yourself! You're a full blown addict!" She started to sob uncontrollably.

Sean pulled her into himself. "Don't cry, sis," he pleaded. "I'm able to manage it. I'll be fine!"

Tiffany pushed herself away and stared at him in helpless frustration. "That's a lie from the pit of hell!" she argued. "Satan has you right where he wants you. When you think you can 'manage' your addiction, you are blinded to truth. It's a 'hook' that Satan puts in you to keep you on his line. Well let me tell you something, Sean, unless you get help, you will never be clean."

"I'll get help! I'll get therapy!" He kissed on her cheek. "I promise."

She bolted upright. "I'll give you one week to get into a program for addiction or I'm going to dad. Agreed?"

Sean nodded remorsefully. "Agreed."

* * *

SIX

The incessant tropical heat of South Florida along with the afternoon thunderstorm elevated Randy's anxiety to new heights as he drove Sean's car home. Tension in the family was growing exponentially and he had no way of controlling it. The Bible passage, "Be anxious for nothing…"went through his mind, but he found it hard to enter into that promise now. *My world seems to be caving in. How can I not be anxious?*

He looked into the rearview mirror to see Lester trailing behind him in his car. *Thanks, Lord for giving our church such a servant. I wonder if he knows what's going on? I can trust him, that much I know.*

They arrived at the Bradshaw home.

"Tiffany home already?" Lester asked, spotting her car in the driveway. "I thought she got home from school at around 4 o'clock?"

Randy opened up Lester's car door then said, "She must've missed a class." He paused then: "I'll just go in and check on Sean, then I'll come out and you can drive me back to the church."

"Okay, pastor," Lester replied and turned off his windshield wipers as Randy walked up to the house.

What's this? The Post Office left a small box on the ground. Randy picked it up and looked at it. It was addressed to Sean from some firm in Canada. He tucked it under his arm and walked into the kitchen with it.

"Hi, dad," Tiffany said while clearing the dishwasher.

He slid the box onto the counter then turned to Tiffany. "Sean still sleeping?"

"He woke up and called Cindy to pick him up. Something about studying with her for their exams."

Randy nodded in surprise. "I had Lester drive him home because he was not feeling well. Did you talk to him? Was he okay?"

"Yeah. Whatever he had must have passed after he slept for a few hours," she replied. "He seemed fine when he left."

"Well, that's good." He walked over to her and hugged her. "Lester is going to drive me back to the church. Mom and I will see you later for dinner."

As he walked out the thought that they both exchanged half-truths never occurred to either one of them.

* * *

Plantation Acres boasted of large estate homes ranging from 3,500 to over 10,000 square feet in gated communities. Most of these homeowners had regularly scheduled housekeepers and landscapers. Manicured lawns and high-end cars in this neighborhood were a familiar sight to Sean and he enjoyed calling on Cindy frequently, especially since her parents liked him knowing he considered her to be just a good friend. That friendship included partnering at school and occasional church functions as well as dining out and visiting movie houses, but with little romantic interest. Her parents believed she was *safe* with him.

With a GPA of 3.95, Cindy was no fool and took her education seriously since her parents demanded she pay half her tuition. No problem for her. She believed God had called her to be a testimony to the world and lived her life as a tribute to her parents that she loved and respected very much. Holding a part-time job at a retail store exposed her to the public where she could say a word in season that would honor the relationship she had with Jesus. She was that kind of person. Wholesome, personable, perky and attractive were her outward attributes while inwardly she was a girl of conviction who screened her thoughts and actions in the light of God's Word. This brought wisdom way beyond her years. Sensing this, Sean sought her for companionship and counsel.

"Run this by me one more time," she said suspiciously while they sat at a table on her covered patio. "You're telling me that you found yourself at home, in your bed, and that you have no idea how you got there? Then your sister comes and tells you that she found you out—that you're on drugs? Am I right so far?"

Sean nodded sheepishly. "That's why I called you so that I could get some advice from somebody outside my family. Somebody neutral," he pleaded.

She unwittingly put her hands on her hips. "Then you told me that Tiffany accused you of shooting up cocaine after you claimed you were taking testosterone injections. Then she demanded you get therapy, right?"

Sean swallowed hard and simply nodded.

She looked at him inquiringly. "Let me ask you something, Sean, and I need you to be totally honest. To me, your answer tells me who you really are." She pointed up and added, "Before God, can you tell me that you are a true Christian?"

Sean squirmed in his seat and rubbed his arms unintentionally, managing to appear unjustly accused, and slightly offended. "I believe I am," he replied. "After all, I am really involved in my dad's church."

Cindy shook her head. "Since when did 'involvement' in any church set the standard for being a Christian?" To her, this was critical information for any advice she might offer. "Can you recall any time in the past when you made a decision to receive Christ as your Savior?"

Sean realized he wasn't going to get away with anything with Cindy. *You're really putting my feet to the fire! Remember, I'm a pastor's son!* He believed he was in the crosshairs and being targeted on a subject that made him uncomfortable. "I was at youth camp eight years ago and made a decision then," he struggled to choke out.

"Did you ever hear the portion in the Bible where it says you're the temple of the Holy Spirit and that you are not to pollute that temple?" she pressed.

Sean shrugged his shoulders and said nothing. Then he suddenly stood up from the table and pointed his finger at her. "Why are you judging me? I came here for some advice and all that I'm getting is a 'grilling.' You're interrogating me!"

"Sit down, Sean!" she demanded, fully expecting his response as a classic diversionary tactic. "And let's be clear about this, mister. If you came here for a 'stroking' to soothe your conscience or to downplay your sister's verdict, you're wrong. You are at a crossroad that can very well determine what you do with the rest of your life." *And your eternal life as well*, she didn't add.

He mechanically sat down starring at the floor, hands in his pockets. He gave a long theatrical sigh then said, "Obviously I'm not going to get any help from you so I might as well be on my way."

Cindy impulsively reached over and grabbed his hand. "Sean, don't you want to be sure of your salvation? Don't leave here without praying with me, please!"

Sean's eye flashed at what he believed was an insult. "You're really getting on my last nerve!" he growled. "I need to go!" He stood up and started for her front door then abruptly stopped short. "I don't have my car here. Can you give me a ride to my friend George's apartment?"

Tears welled up in her eyes. She grabbed her handbag off the table then beckoned to him. "Let's go."

* * *

Tiffany looked through the window over the kitchen sink to see her mother stepping out of a car she didn't recognize at first. Seconds later Stephanie emerged from the driver's side. *This is good*, she realized. *We should talk.*

"Smells good, Tiff," Laurie announced as she walked in the front door with Stephanie trailing behind. "What's cooking?"

Tiffany met her mother with a hug. "Found a tray of lasagna in the freezer when I got home. Plenty for Stephanie too."

"I love Italian!" Stephanie said, smiling luminously.

"Dad's on his way home," Laurie noted. She pointed down the hallway. "Sean in his room?"

Tiffany turned away. "I dropped him at Cindy's house. I think they're studying together."

Laurie scratched her head. "He didn't take his own car?"

"He wasn't feeling so good so I drove him over to her house," Tiffany replied. *Mom, stop the questions, please.*

"The flu is going around," Stephanie said casually. "Seems like everybody's getting it." They all moaned softly.

Tiffany needed to take control. "You like garlic on your Italian bread, Stephanie?"

Laurie took the cue. Glancing down at the table she said, "Let me help you get the dinner out."

Fifteen minutes later Randy came home.

Laurie met him at the front door with a hug and a peck on his cheek. "Surprise! Tiffy made the dinner."

He peeked into the kitchen. "That's up there with Moses parting the Red Sea," he teased.

"Ha, ha," Tiffany laughed. "Wash up, dad, dinner's ready in five minutes."

He turned the corner and spotted Stephanie. He saluted her and said, "Doing all right young lady?"

She looked up at him with a broad smile and gave him a Boy Scout salute in return. "Doing well, pastor."

Randy looked down toward Sean's bedroom. "Any word from Sean?"

"Give him a call and see if he plans on coming home for dinner," Laurie suggested.

"Right," Randy replied and walked off into the living room with the wireless house phone. He failed to notice that Tiffany followed him with her eyes.

Seconds later Sean's cell ringtone sounded out a tune from U2. He read the Caller ID and pressed *Answer*. "Hello, dad," he said.

"Your mother wants to know if you're coming home for dinner. Tiffy heated up the lasagna."

"Umm—" a momentary pause, then: "I'm still studying at Cindy's house and we're going to get some pizza. I'll be home later."

"You doing all right, Sean?" Randy whispered conspiratorially.

"I'll be fine, dad," he replied.

Relieved: "Good, I'll see you later." Randy clicked off then turned toward the kitchen. "Sean is eating over Cindy's. More for us."

"Who was that?" George asked as he walked into his TV room carrying two cans of beer.

"My dad. Wanted to know how I'm doing."

"You told him you're doing great, right?" George said, handing him the beer.

Sean nodded and said, "Yeah, I'm doing great." He slugged down the beer.

George smirked and then handed him a small bag of white pills. "Time to travel to new heights, bro."

Sean pulled back to look at him and scanned his face. For a split-second he thought he saw the face of a demon on George. *Must be the beer.*

* * *

"That was a great meal," Stephanie remarked, pushing herself away from the dinner table.

Randy lifted his coffee cup in the air. "Kudos, Tiffy."

"Just a reminder, mom made the lasagna, Tiffy just heated it up," Laurie noted with a chuckle.

"All glory goes to mom on this," Tiffany replied graciously then turned to her mother. "Why don't you and dad go relax on the patio while Stephanie and I clean up and load the dishwasher."

"Sounds like a plan!" Laurie replied and gestured to Randy to follow her out to the patio. Dad and Mom walked off hand-in-hand.

"When the dessert is ready, I'll call you guys back in," Tiffany added.

Tiffany grabbed several plates off the table and signaled Stephanie to do the same. Stephanie took the cue and followed her. "What's up?" Stephanie said. "I can read your mind. You're bummed about something."

Tiffany loaded the dishes in the dishwasher then walked to get her pocketbook while Stephanie looked on. She took the white caplet out of her pocketbook and handed it to her. "In your past you've been exposed to people on drugs, well I need your opinion on something. "What is this pill?" she asked trenchantly.

Stephanie examined the caplet very carefully. She looked for an imprint then smelled it, and finally touched it with her moist finger and held the residue up to the light. "I've seen unmarked pills like this before. My guess is that it's oxycodone, 500 milligrams."

"Oh, no!" Tiffany exclaimed. She unwittingly backed herself into one of the kitchen chairs and plopped down into it. "I took that pill from Sean's pocket," she lamented as she shook her head. "He's become a drug addict."

Stephanie blinked in disbelief. "Now wait a minute," she said. "I can't be sure that it is oxycodone. And besides, how do you know he's taking these?"

"He has a whole packet full of those pills. And I can bet they are oxycodone and not ibuprofen or acetaminophen."

"If he's addicted to these, he's in deep trouble," Stephanie advised ruefully.

"And that's just the half of it. He's also on cocaine."

Stephanie squeezed her eyes shut momentarily. "How do you know he's on cocaine?"

"Because I confronted him and saw the track marks on his arms. Once I accused him, he admitted it to me. He promised to get therapy because I threatened to go to dad and mom with it."

"This is very serious, Tiffy. He needs to get help right away. The combination of these two substances is a heavy habit and extremely harmful."

Tiffany put her finger to her temple. "I'm wondering where he gets these pills from? Who is supplying him with these?" She blinked several times then walked over to the counter and picked up the box addressed to Sean and read the large print on the return address label. "This is postmarked from Canada. From 'Maple Leaf Products.'" She shook the box then bounced it up and down in her hand. It didn't rattle but was relatively weighty. "This could be from one of those Canadian drug dealers that fill up my Internet spam folder every day. You know, the illegal market."

Stephanie took the box from her and looked closely at the return label. "In the small print it says that Maple Leaf Products are rare coin dealers." She looked quizzically at Tiffany. "Is Sean into rare coins?"

"If he is, no one in this family knows about it," she replied sarcastically. "It's probably a front organization for getting illegal drugs into the States."

Stephanie nodded in agreement. "This is much bigger than you and I, Tiffy," she realized numbly. "We need to go to your father with this."

Tiffany threw her hands up in the air. "I can't. I made an agreement with Sean that I wouldn't go to our parents if he went for therapy. So we need to wait it out and see if he keeps his end of the deal."

I know from experience that drug addicts don't keep deals. "And if he doesn't keep the deal and goes to the next step . . ." she hesitated and stared at her.

" . . . and overdoses," Tiffany completed her sentence as a tear appeared in her eye.

"That is the awful end game of drug addiction," Stephanie summarized as she replaced the box on the counter.

"What else can I do but to leave this on the altar with God," Tiffany said dolefully.

"If that's the way the Lord is leading you," Stephanie replied, "than that's what you should do." *But I am not bound by that agreement*, she didn't say.

Tiffany dried her eye with a napkin then took a deep breath. "I'll call dad and mom in for dessert." The rest of the evening went as planned without interruption.

* * *

Susan walked into Randy's office carrying a tray with four coffee mugs and a box of donuts and then placed it on the table in front of the leather sofa and sat down. "Coffee and donuts, gentlemen," she said. "Pastor's treat."

Rick Kelly's face lit up as he reached over and grabbed a donut and a mug while Mike and Lester sat on the end of the sofa in silence. "Dig in Mike, Lester," Randy bade them cordially.

"Maybe later," Lester replied while Mike just held up a hand. Randy blinked at the responses and perceived undercurrents were swirling about.

"Our staff meeting this week is about redirecting my sermon focus here at Plantation Gate," Randy began. "I plan to give a series of sermons that will disarm any visitors and embrace those members who think the Christian Church at large is too critical or judgmental—even too legalistic—if you will. I've spoken to a number of pastors in our local association and they have had great success and growth by preaching to the needs people already feel and then in turn point them to a deep need and God's provision of the Gospel.

He leaned toward his staff and added, "We need to bring the church up to modern times and not by preaching 'fire and brimstone' from the pulpit any more. Those times are gone forever. What we need today is to point people to the cross and let God do the rest. And the way we do it is to find out what their needs are and show them how God can help them manage those needs." He stopped and looked at their faces. Rick was nodding along with Susan, but he sensed Lester and Mike held a different opinion. If there was any disparate at all, it was coming from Mike with Lester in tow behind him. "What say you, Mike?"

Mike crossed his arms and said, "I might be the odd man out here, but this plan sounds to me like we're going the way of the liberal church and addressing the felt need of the visitors and congregation." He shook his head. "I too have done some reading and the problem of preaching to felt needs is that our 'needs' are hopelessly confused, even hidden from us. The knowledge of our deepest needs is a secret even to ourselves until we receive that knowledge by the work of the Holy Spirit and the gift of the Scriptures. Add to that, our perceived or felt needs almost always turn out to be something other than *needs*—at least in any serious sense.

"We all have wants and desires and concerns, but most of these are not genuine needs that lead to desperation—the kind of needs that remind us constantly that we lack all self-sufficiency. Actually, to the contrary, most of us feel quite self-sufficient. Therefore, the needs we feel are the *needs* characteristic of apathetic affluence, romantic aspirations, and spiritual emptiness.

"I've dug into this subject and to paraphrase Albert Mohler, he said that preachers who believe they can move the attention of individuals from their 'felt needs' to their need for the Gospel will find, inevitably, that the distance between the individual and the Gospel has not been reduced by attention to lesser needs. From a personal perspective, I believe the sinner's need for Christ is a need unlike all other needs—and the satisfaction of having other needs stroked and affirmed is often a hindrance to the sinner's understanding of the Gospel." He paused when he saw Randy tighten his lips but believed he had to get his point off his chest. "Jesus doesn't meet our needs, he rearranges them. He cares very little about most things that we assume are our needs, and he gives us needs we would never have had if we hadn't met Him. Jesus reorders our needs. Most of the people in the church I know get their needs met without prayer. So they've moved on to 'needs' like a good sex life, a satisfying career, an enjoyable vacation, a positive outlook on life, and the stuff the Bible has absolutely no interest in."

Randy felt rebuked. He took a sip of his coffee then looked at Lester to gage his response. Lester's physiognomy said it all. He agreed with Mike. He turned to Rick and Susan who shrugged their shoulders. "Well, as far as I'm concerned—" He stopped short as his cell phone vibrated. He checked the Caller ID. It was Sean. He ignored the call. " . . . I appreciate your input, Mike, and to a degree I agree with you, but you can't knock success, and the pastor's I've polled tell me their churches are booming with seekers and their numbers are really climbing, so it can't be all that bad. Obviously God is blessing this new wave."

"Pastor, we're not going this direction to attract deep pockets, are we?" Lester asked.

"With our new building, we have a steep mortgage payment, I grant you that, Lester, but that is secondary. Don't we all want the church to grow?" he argued. "Of course we do. So if we have to modify our message somewhat in order to meet the 'needs' of the community, is that so wrong?"

Mike shifted his weight on the sofa. He felt uncomfortable. "It is wrong if this philosophy of ministry leads us down the slippery slope toward postmodernism and other offshoots of orthodox Christianity that challenges and questions the Word of God and the Bible's plan of salvation."

Lester clucked reprovingly. "I hear there is a lot of that going around."

Postmodernism, Randy thought. *I know the danger in that. I've held out against it. But we need to try different things in order for our church to survive. For now, I must get Mike on board if my plan to move the church forward is to work the way I had hoped.* "If we just implement this on a trial basis, can I expect your support, Mike? Lester?"

Mike knew he had to answer to God and to the congregation if questioned. He had to speak his mind now, not after the fact. "In my purview, I see many of these churches that have adopted these latest 'trends' have morphed from being a ministry to becoming a *business*.

With sky-high mortgage payments due to their building campaigns, they are concerned with the numbers. The number of attendees, and the number of dollars coming into the collection plates, when we should be concerned with people's souls, not their pocketbooks."

"That's never going to happen here at Plantation Gate," Randy said with clear precision.

"Well, the day we bring in disco lights and start dancing in the sanctuary is my last day here," Mike said sarcastically.

"Mike, when you make a joke, you drop a bombsight," Randy teased to lighten the mood in the room.

"As long as we don't take sin off the table, pastor, I can go along with you for the time being," Lester allowed, nodding at Mike.

Mike threw his hands up in mock surrender. "Let's try it out to see if it flies."

Randy's cell phone vibrated once more. He checked the Caller ID to see it was Sean again. "I have to take this call." The staff walked out leaving him with the notion they approved of his trial plan.

He walked to the window and pressed *Answer*. "Dad, this is Sean. I'm running a little late, but I'll be there in time for Sunday worship. Please tell the youth group I'm on my way."

Randy's heart sunk. His face suddenly flushed as his anxiety level soared. "Sean, today is Wednesday, not Sunday. And besides that, you didn't come home last night. What's going on?"

A pause, then: "Oh, I guess I got my days mixed up. Sorry. After studying with Cindy I had her drop me at George's apartment and we got involved in a movie so I slept over at his place. I'll see you later." *Click.*

Randy squeezed his eyes shut. *This is getting serious.*

* * *

Stephanie carried over two coffees and two pumpkin muffins to the table at Plantation café and sat down while Tiffany checked her emails on her cell phone. "Anything interesting?" Stephanie asked.

"Two emails from Alex and one from a girlfriend from school," she replied.

"How's Alex these days?"

"He's doing well. We've been missing each other because he's been working with the pastor at Providence and cramming for exams as well. We'll catch up this weekend."

"He seems like a nice young man," Stephanie said with a luminous smile. "And from what I hear he has a tight relationship with Jesus. You can't go wrong when the man you plan to marry is dedicated to the Lord."

"I hear that," she replied. *Ringtone.* Tiffany glanced down at her phone then hesitated fractionally. "Oh, oh. It's my dad," she said nervously.

"Tiffy, I just got a call from your brother . . ." he paused, then " . . . he sounded, well, he sounded confused," Stephanie heard. "He's over at George's apartment and I think he may have been drinking. I'm tied up here at church and I'd rather your mother didn't know about this, so can you scoot over there and check on him?"

Tiffany instantly gazed off at a fixed object to assemble her response when suddenly Stephanie nodded and gestured to her. "Say yes," she whispered.

"Sure, dad. Don't worry, he'll be fine," she said in disbelief. "I'll call you later," she added before disconnecting.

Stephanie grabbed her car keys off the table and said, "Let's get moving! This doesn't sound good." Then they threw the coffee and muffins in the waste container.

"I'll drive," Tiffany said as they hurried into the parking lot. "I know where George lives."

Stephanie nodded then handed over her keys as they slid into her car. "What kind of person is this George?"

Tiffany tried to calm her fears but they took hold of her. She accelerated too fast out of the parking lot and careened into a curb before entering into the street. "Oh, no—" she used a vile word—"not a flat tire!"

"We're okay," Stephanie said, looking out the window. "You're fine, just slow down."

Tiffany reflexively reduced her speed. "This George is a real sleaze ball," she finally replied with a shake of the head. "I really don't know what Sean sees in this loser. He knows him from college, but he's a real burn out as far as I'm concerned."

"Does this George do drugs?"

Tiffany clenched the steering wheel and noted, "Every time I've seen him he looks like he's high on something."

"Just trying to prepare myself for what I think is going to be a sticky situation," Stephanie replied gloomily. "We're going to really need the Lord to help us on this one."

"'The Lord will fight for us, we need only to be still,'" Tiffany quoted.

"Good one," Stephanie affirmed.

Minutes later they were at George Mason's apartment complex.

* * *

Junked cars along with overflowing garbage dumpsters littered the parking lot at Sunview Apartments. The roof looked in need of dire repair and the paint on the walls was peeling off. The guardrails on the apartment patios were strewn with drying clothing and many of the patios were used for excess storage, cluttered with boxes. The area was notorious for drugs and prostitution. "These are not high end living quarters," Stephanie remarked as they drove through the parking lot. *It's the kind of place someone would go to commit suicide,* she thought.

"Over there," Tiffany said, pointing to a first floor apartment with an old bike on the patio and Christmas lights dangling from the ceiling. "I dropped Sean here one time and I remember the lights."

"This is going to be rich," Stephanie noted dryly. She pointed to the Christmas lights as they walked up to the complex and added, "Sam Knowles from Homeless Outreach always used to say that when he saw Christmas lights on homes out of season it was a sign of trouble in the home. And you know what, he was right."

Tiffany grabbed a bag she took from the house off the front seat then motioned to Stephanie to follow her. At the apartment Tiffany lifted the doorknocker and banged it down several times. As she did four cockroaches scooted out from under the door and fled. "I hate those things. They really nauseate me," she said in disgust.

"I have a feeling we're going to see a two-legged cockroach open this door," Stephanie quipped. Then she put her hand over the viewing port on the door. "I want this to be a surprise."

Seconds later: "Go away!" they heard through the door.

Tiffany shook her head. The voice was not Sean's. "This is not going to be a surprise." Then she lifted the doorknocker again and with greater force banged it four times, then kicked the bottom of the door. "OPEN UP, SEAN!" she screamed. "I KNOW YOU'RE IN THERE!"

The door opened slowly and a foul odor wafted out and smacked the girls in the face. "Whew! What is that smell!?" Stephanie exclaimed between gasps. *It smells like cat urine!*

George immediately recognized Tiffany. He made no apology for the putrid stink as he opened the door. Once he opened the door three cats scooted out between his legs. "Sean is sleeping now," he said sheepishly.

"I need to speak to him now, George!" she demanded as she pushed the door open fully.

George backed up to let them in and then bowed mockingly. "My home is your home."

Stephanie held her nose as she walked in and cast her eyes in all directions. The apartment reminded her of an unkempt hobbit hovel void of any sanitary or dietary laws. Posters of rock stars known to be potheads who died of drug overdoses lined the walls. Soiled towels and clothes were piled in the corners [she believed the cats used them for beds] and on the kitchen table were empty cans of soup and baked beans, along with empty pizza cartons. A host of empty beer cans were assembled into pyramids on the counter while the crushed ones occupied the sink. Next to the refrigerator was a cat litter box that apparently had not been cleaned in months. "Where is he?" she snapped.

"Huh?" he said disjointedly. He teetered to one side then added, "Tiffany I know—"but who are you?" Apparently he was high on something as his eyes were bloodshot and he garbled his words.

"Never mind, pal! I'm with Tiffany!" she snarled. "And you're lucky I'm not with the police."

George blinked several times when he heard 'police' and said as he gestured, "He's in the back bedroom." Moments later they heard the front door open and close as he went out to fetch the cats.

The hallway connecting the bedroom was darkened. Tiffany threw on the light switch then looked at the fixture. "Bulb burned out," she said. "Figures."

As they walked by the bathroom Stephanie pushed the door open to let some light into the hallway. She shot a look into the bathroom and was repulsed by the squalor. "This is a snake pit," she whispered.

The bedroom door was ajar so Tiffany nudged it and it slowly opened. They were not prepared for what they saw. "Oh my God!" Tiffany said as her breath caught in her throat. Stephanie just covered her mouth with her hand in sheer disbelief.

Sean looked unconscious and about to slide out of a folding beach chair that was next to a bed. He was only in his underwear and his mouth hung open while breathing in shallow drafts. His arms with palms up were stretched out in front of him. Stephanie walked to him and saw fresh injection sores on his arms. "Here's the culprit," she said as she bent down and picked up a hypodermic syringe off the floor. She held it up in the air. "Cocaine," she said ruefully.

Tiffany started to wretch her guts. "I'm going to be sick!" she exclaimed and turned away to step outside of the room. Moments later with her handkerchief over her mouth she walked over to her brother and slapped him across the face. "Wake up, Sean!" she shouted. "You're not going to die a drug addict!"

Sean's eyes fluttered as Tiffany prepared to slam him again. "Where am I?" he choked out. He immediately reached over and grabbed a pillow off the bed to cover himself and gazed at Stephanie. He rubbed his eyes as he started to come around and then tried to focus on her face. "Stephanie? What are you doing here?"

"Your father called your sister to come and get you out of this garbage dumpster," she replied. "I came along to help her out, and you know what?"

Dazed and shaking his head. "No, what?"

"She really needed me here. You're a mess, Sean, and you need help."

Tiffany returned from the bathroom with a cup of water. "Here, drink this," she said forcefully and shoved the cup into his hand. Some of the water dripped from his mouth as he attempted to stand up. Tiffany gently pushed him back into the chair then pulled the box out of the bag she had been carrying. She glanced at Stephanie then said to Sean, "Tell me what's in this box."

Sean paused momentarily then nibbled on his lower lip. "They're coins from Canada."

"Oh, really? Well I've got a hunch that they're not." She thrust the box into his lap. "Open it!"

He looked around the room then shrugged his shoulders. Stephanie followed his eyes then reached over to the dresser where an empty bottle of wine stood and picked up the corkscrew and handed it to him. "Here, use this."

Reluctantly he slashed the packing tape and slowly pulled out a small bubble wrap pocket with two coins in it. "See, behold, coins from Canada," he snapped.

Stephanie snatched the bubble wrap pocket from him and inspected the coins. They were Canadian but mere five-cent coins. "Who are you kidding?!" she said with a derisive snort. Then she pulled the box out of his hands and dug her fingernails into the bottom of the box and lifted out a cardboard liner. Under the liner was a sandwich bag filled with white caplets. "A-hah!" she cried out. "What have we here?"

"You're disgusting!" Tiffany yelled out. "How could *you* do this?" She pulled the white caplet from her handbag and compared it to the ones in the sandwich bag Stephanie was holding. "This is oxycodone. Just like the one I found in your pants."

He overlooked her accusation and sat erect in the chair. "Well, sis," he replied with one hand on his hip, "how could you do what you did?"

Tiffany exchanged looks with Stephanie. "What are you talking about, Sean?"

A devilish grin came over his face. "How could you get pregnant by Alex and not be ashamed? After all, you must be having sex with him. Have you told dad and mom yet?" He scanned her up and down. "You're looking hefty."

Tiffany backed up two paces as adrenaline swept through her body like a flash flood. "You're out of your mind, Sean!" she argued. "This is the drugs talking!" She looked at Stephanie then back at Sean and added, "How dare you attack me!"

"This is what happens when you confront a drug addict," Stephanie explained to them both. "To avoid dealing with one's own culpability—attack the critic. I've seen it many times when working with the homeless addicts." Sean looked at her with a queer expression like he was being misunderstood.

Ringtone. Tiffany pulled her cell phone from her handbag and read the Caller ID. "Oh, great, it's dad."

"Let me talk to him," Sean said with a sardonic grin.

Stephanie shook her head. "No way," she said and motioned for Tiffany to leave the room.

Tiffany pressed *Answer* and walked out of the room with the phone to her ear. "We're here at George's," she said, "Sean was sleeping it off when we got here. We'll get him cleaned up and bring him home." Seconds later she walked back into the room. "I've saved your butt once more, my brother, but you are on my last nerve."

He started to stand up but Stephanie pushed him back into the chair. "We're not interested in seeing your private parts, bub."

Sean grinned and held out his hand. "I want my pills back."

Tiffany ignored his plea, took the bag from Stephanie and spun around and rushed to the bathroom and flushed the caplets down the toilet and marched back into the bedroom. "Have you seen anybody about getting the therapy you agreed to?" she demanded.

He slouched down in the chair. "I've made some calls," he replied blandly.

"That's a no!" Stephanie declared. "He's lying."

With her hands balled at her sides she looked Sean in the eyes and said, "Where's the cocaine you're shooting up?"

A frosty silence, then his eyes flicked to her face, then away. He looked guilty. "I don't have any more."

"And what about your 'looser' friend, George?" Stephanie put in.

"I don't think he has any more either," he smiled, a sphinxlike smile.

"Probably has some stashed someplace in this dump," Stephanie concluded. She turned to Tiffany. "We need to get him out of here, pronto."

"We'll wait outside this room while you get dressed, Sean." Then she shook her finger at him. "And don't try any funny business. You here me?" she instructed clearly.

He simply nodded as they walked out.

"I'm this close to calling the police on this sleaze bag," Tiffany said, holding up her thumb and index finger one inch apart as they stood by the front door.

"The only problem in calling the police on George is that it will involve Sean," Stephanie replied. "And I don't think that would fare well with your dad and mom."

"I suppose you're right," Tiffany added as an afterthought. "So what should we do?"

"I'm thinking that we need to get your father involved in this without the authorities," she said. "After all, it *is* his son."

"I'm afraid of what the outcome would be," Tiffany said torpidly.

"But—" she paused and shook her head, "…if you wait too long—and I've seen this happen before—Sean can slip over the cliff into the pit of serious drug addiction and it is near impossible to pull them out without professional intervention."

"It seems to me that he's just about there already," Tiffany said in somber tones.

"I'm ready, sis," they heard as Sean walked down the hallway, combing his hair. She gave him a look of revulsion.

As they opened the door they spotted George sitting on a nearby bench on a grassy knoll holding one of his cats, gazing at them. "A curse on you, you little weasel!" Tiffany yelled out. "The Lord should give you a double portion of pain!"

Stephanie held Sean by the arm and escorted him to the car as Tiffany paused momentarily to take a photo of George with her iPhone. *Just for the record.*

* * *

"You know that I love you and your family, Tiffany, so don't mind me if I ask, what's all this about you being pregnant?" Stephanie began after looking to see Sean sleeping in the rear seat.

Tiffany felt a kindred spirit toward Stephanie. She had confided in her before and was given good godly counsel. She could trust her. "Truthfully, we've been having sex," she admitted. "Afterward we go to God and confess our fornication, but weeks later we fall into it again." She turned and started crying. With eyes pleading: "I really love him, and he loves me, so is this so wrong?"

Stephanie took a deep breath in hopes for a quick flash of divine wisdom. Solomon she was not, but truth spoken in love is hard to refuse. "I can only tell you what God says," she explained. "All sex outside of marriage is sin. That's the cold truth. But the Lord knows your heart and treats it just as he would any other sin. If you really want God's blessing in your relationship, you'll do things God's way. That means you abstain until you're married. If not—" she paused, "—then you just take your chances."

She rubbed her tummy. "I'm still getting my period so I can't be pregnant, but I don't understand why I'm gaining so much weight."

"You should go to a doctor and find out."

"I'm a little afraid of what he might say," she replied.

"'Fear not little flock, for it is your Father's good pleasure to give you the kingdom'," Stephanie quoted.

Tiffany smiled at her. "Thanks. I needed that."

Sean groaned and then curled up in a fetal position in the back seat.

Stephanie glanced over at him then brought up the subject again. "Do you have a plan on how to handle your brother? I mean are you going to bring your parents into this?"

"I'm still bound by the promise I made to Sean that I wouldn't go to our parents if he went for therapy or counseling," she replied. "So I think I should give him more time."

Stephanie nodded and grew thoughtful. "I see," she said. *But I am not bound by that promise. Time is the one thing you cannot afford when your brother's life is at stake.*

* * *

SEVEN

As Stephanie drove up to Plantation Gate church she noticed the wording on the church's sign had been changed. It listed the upcoming sermon title: *Christ Can Meet All Your Needs. Come and See How.* The hours of the worship services were listed under the title. *Nice provocative title*, she thought. *I wonder what Pastor Randy means by the catchy title?*

"Pastor's wife not in yet?" she asked Susan as she walked into the church office.

"Laurie said she needed to pick up some church supplies and would be a little late," Susan replied with a nod.

Stephanie looked over at the telephone console then at her wristwatch. *He's not on the phone and it's still early in the morning. Is this a divine opportunity, Lord?* "I need to speak to Pastor Randy, Susan, so if there are any calls for me, just take a message." With that she walked promptly to his office.

Randy spotted her at the doorway. "Hey, Steph, come on in," he said with a broad smile taking notice of her colorful dress. Stephanie walked in and sat in one of his stuffed 'counseling' chairs adjacent to his desk and crossed her legs. "Before I forget, I wanted to thank you for helping Tiffy fetch Sean last night. I guess you guys stopped off someplace and doused him with coffee because when he got home he looked fine. Thanks again."

No comment. Then after an acknowledging bob: "I need some counseling, pastor," she said. "A friend of mine has a real problem and I need some godly advice on how to minister to her."

"Tell me about this person," he replied and pulled up another chair in front of her.

"Well, I know this young lady intern that works with me down at the homeless shelter who confided in me that she started out socially drinking with her friends and then experimented with recreational drugs, you know, the marijuana and stuff, and then when her schooling—she is in college—became too demanding, she needed more of a kick so she started snorting cocaine.

"She fell in with the wrong crowd and instead of them helping her out of the hell hole she found herself, they dragged her deeper by injecting cocaine and adding oxycodone to her menu. Let me add that she's a functional addict but appears to be worsening."

"Does this young lady know the Lord?" Randy asked. "Because that is the starting place for recovery. Christ is able to deliver from any form of addiction."

"She claims to be a Christian," Stephanie replied. "But there is only a limited amount of evidence to support that claim."

Randy sat listening intently while starring at some imaginary spot in the air. His brow furrowed. "Go on."

"As a friend and colleague, I threatened to go to the director and report her unless she sought help and she agreed, but did not follow through with the agreement and just recently I learned that she is now a serious addict in need of intervention."

"Does she have any family?" he asked. "Is there somebody else beside you that can help her?"

Stephanie fixed on him with a penetrating stare. "Her family hold very respected positions in the community and I'm afraid to go to them for fear that the revelation that their daughter is a drug addict may really hurt their reputation and radically impact on their involvement in the community." She stopped and looked at him squarely. "What would you do?"

Randy nodded then meditated on the matter. Then after a moment of deep thought: "Every effort needs to be made to protect this young lady's life. Apparently this gal is now incapable of helping herself—she's in too deep. Outside help is now required. If that means the family must be brought in to help, then that's what needs to be done. The issue of reputation needs to be secondary. I don't think waiting is an option because drug addiction can increase exponentially with disastrous results for everybody. What you don't want is for her to OD. If that happens everybody loses and will live with regrets for the rest of their lives!"

Stephanie stood up and walked to the window, peeked through the blinds into the rear yard then turned to him. "Randy, the character in this story I just told you is fictitious." She walked over to him then put her hand on his shoulder and said, "Take hold of yourself, Randy. I'm talking about *your* son, Sean. He is a serious drug addict."

Silence.

The realization crashed in on him. Flashbacks of Sean's erratic behavior suddenly filled his mind. Events and lies scrambled to be heard in his heart. He tried to repress them but the truth knotted in his chest. He stood up next to her. "How do you know all this?"

"Because Tiffany and I went to his friend George's apartment and caught him red-handed," she said. "He wasn't drunk as you thought, but high on cocaine and oxycodone." She sighed and added, "Tiffany has known about this for quite a while, but she made a promise to him that she would not tell you and Laurie if he got help."

"And—?"

"He lied like most addicts do. He never went for help." She patted his shoulder and added, "But I am not bound by Tiffany's pledge and know the magnitude of the problem, that's why I have come to you."

Randy stood up and turned to her. He was visibly shaken. There was weariness in his expression of the worn-down look of a man living with a multitude of regrets. A wave of despair suddenly swept over him. *Failure. Hypocrisy. Alone.* "I don't know…" he fumbled for words, "… how to solve this. Can you help me?" He began to weep.

"You need to go before the Lord and ask for wisdom before doing anything else," she instructed firmly. "Then go to Laurie and discuss this together. Then formulate a plan and trust the Lord to honor it. Be sure that I will be praying for you and Laurie." Then she shook her head. "The one thing you don't want to do is to prolong taking action." With that she turned on her heel and walked out of the office.

An interminable period seemed to pass as he sat there with his head bowed and tears dripping from his eyes. *Lord, I don't know if I can go to Laurie with this now. I feel alone and discarded by you. Where are you in all of this? Help!* He stood up and mechanically walked around his desk. Thoughts of one of his seminary professor's crisis came to his mind. During one of his lectures this professor shared with the class his recent experience. He had a doctorate in theology and was tenured at Wheaton and during one of his teachings he suddenly collapsed. He was taken to the hospital and diagnosed with a nervous breakdown. He was put on medical leave and after two months he garnered enough strength to go back to work—not as a seminary professor—but as an employee at Home Depot's garden center.

There he remained in 'exile' if you will for several weeks until a colleague telephoned him and asked, "Are you ready to go back to teaching? If you are, I have a spot for you."

This broken man reluctantly agreed and when he re-appeared before his class made an astounding observation of his experience. He related to the class that mankind seeks to have any difficulty resolved quickly if not immediately, but the Lord above is not interested in how quickly we go from point A to point B. He is only interested in the *process*. That doesn't mean he doesn't' hear our prayers. How we handle a crisis or tragedy is what matters to God, not the instant remedy. When the infrastructure of our lives we have built crumbles, to what and to whom do we go? In the final analysis, the only resolution of any major crisis is always 'vertical,' between you and your God. He is the God of detail and the only One who can bring us out of the dilemma. And until we recognize that, the *process* continues.

Yea, Lord, I remember. He sat down at his desk, slipped his shoes off and leaned back in his chair with his hands behind his head. *Every life that would be strong must have its Holy of Holies into which only God enters. I know this, Lord,* he pondered. He looked around his office reminding himself that he was alone. *There is a strange strength conceived in solitude I am told,* he thought. *Crows go in flocks and wolves in packs, but the lion and the eagle are solitaires. Strength is in quietness,* he realized. *I need to go apart with my Lord, and sit at his feet in sacred privacy of His blessed presence to know what to do.*

He leaned forward, put on his shoes and walked out of his office over to Susan. "Please tell Laurie that I'll be out for several hours. If anyone asks for me, just tell them I'll get back to them."

Susan nodded. "Will do, pastor."

* * *

Nature had a compelling voice in Randy's life. To him the beauty of the Lord in nature often served as a ministry diversion and when a crisis came, a distraction. When he would dwell on its complexity it often gave him perspective in solving deep problems.

He marveled at the enormity and intricacy of the universe and how God managed to keep it functioning like a Swiss watch, complete with accuracy and precision. With humans, he never could understand how the humanist could deny the existence of God when examining the intricacies of the human eye. How the Atheist explained these truths away was to him a mystery wrapped up in a conundrum coated with satanic delusion.

Thoughts of Sean came tumbling in on his deliberations! Help Lord!

He forced himself to travel the short distance to Flamingo Gardens, the botanical wonderland of South Florida that boasted of exotic tropical trees and plants along with an aviary and animal exhibits, and walked to the bench underneath one of the giant banyan trees. He looked at the numerous columns of roots connecting the branches to the ground and shook his head in amazement. *Convoluted, that's what this tree reminds me of.* "God, how do I move forward with this convoluted problem hanging over me?" he whispered aloud. "I'm paralyzed over Sean. It would be different if it were someone else in the congregation who came for counseling. I could easily have given them biblical instruction. Given them biblical principles to act on and godly wisdom to comfort them at a time of need. But this is different. This is my own family—my son. If I have failed him, show me. Am I too involved in this new building? How come I didn't recognize the signs that my son was in trouble? Lord," he begged, "I am weak. I am broken. Help me through this *process.*"

He looked up into the massive leaf canopy offered by the huge tree and then closed his eyes. How long he sat there with his eyes closed he wouldn't remember. But his mind drifted and he felt much of the built-up tension drain from his body. His spirit wanted communion with his God. He knew he desperately needed divine direction and an emotional catharsis. *Be anxious for nothing*, he heard in his heart. *You shall know the truth and the truth will set you free.*

He opened his eyes and heard the mellifluous sound of several mockingbirds sitting on the branches above him. He ran his fingers through his hair then inhaled deeply and then gazed off into the distance. *I will confront Sean, but should I tell Laurie? Can I deal with her heartbreak as well as my own? Should I tell the truth?* he mused. *I don't know if I am able to do that now.*

* * *

Stephanie and Laurie stood side by side at Susan's desk as Randy walked in the door. For a split second as they turned to greet him he felt a moment of sheer panic.

He walked over to Laurie and gave her a hug and said, "I love you." Then he gave Stephanie an apologetic look that she perceived was his way of saying, *I'm sorry if I can't tell her.*

"Got a few minutes, honey?" Laurie asked as she nodded to Susan.

"Of course, babe," he said. Stephanie gave them both a salute and strolled off as Randy and Laurie walked to his office.

"How long have we been married?" she asked as he closed the door behind them.

Randy sat in a stuffed chair and ticked off his fingers as he thought on her motive for the question. "Twenty-five years." He smiled and added, "Twenty-five *beautiful* years!"

"Long enough for me to know my husband and if he's having a problem, right?"

Randy's heart began to beat faster as he closed his eyes and put a palm to his forehead. *Oh God, don't tell me Stephanie said something to her.* "I guess," he answered at first. "Of course!"

"Then tell me what's going on inside your head because when you walked in just now I could read the look on your face. Something is troubling you, and as your wife I want to help you with it."

He was relieved by the nature of the question, but: *Lord, I just don't have the presence of mind to tell her what's really going on,* he reasoned, *and if I did, she will be crushed and our ministry will fail for loss of confidence.* "I'm troubled over Sean. I think he has a drinking problem," he said sadly.

She slowly walked over to the other stuffed chair and sat down and started rubbing her palms together. "How long have you known?"

"I really just discovered it," he explained. "He came to the church yesterday for the youth meeting and was intoxicated. So I had Lester drive him home to sleep it off."

"That explain why he's been avoiding us," she answered. "You know, hanging out over at Cindy's I guess."

"I guess," he agreed halfheartedly.

"You'll talk to him about this?"

"Of course," he replied. "Don't you worry."

* * *

EIGHT

It was 3:30 A.M. when he awoke from his bed with a severe headache. He sat up and rubbed his temples for several minutes to no avail. *Should I take a shower and let the hot water sooth my head?* He didn't know, nor could he know that this was only the beginning of many nighttime headaches that would rob him of sleep.

Whether it was from his sinuses or a migraine, he wasn't sure, but he did know that severe stress brings on headaches, and Sean had become a major stressor in his family.

"You okay?" Laurie asked as she sat up and glanced at the clock. "You tossed and turned for an hour."

"My head is pounding," he replied as he massaged the right side of his head. "Killer headache." He knew within himself that he had been running 'tapes' of Sean every waking moment.

"Can I get you something?" she asked and reached over to turn on the end table lamp.

"I took two pain relievers, but it just won't quit." He stood up. "I'll go sleep on the sofa so as not to disturb you. You go back to sleep."

Laurie turned off the light, dropped back into the bed and rolled over. "I love you."

"Love you too." He grabbed his pillow and walked out of the bedroom to the living room and stretched out on the sofa. *I hate it when I can't sleep at night, that's when my demons come to haunt me.*

* * *

Family stress…headache…interrupted sleep…demons…schedule prayer meeting. Lord, Randy thought, *how much more?* It was now 8: 30 A. M. when he opened the door to the church to Susan's bright smile.

"Good morning, Pastor Randy!" she said cheerfully.

I'm in excruciating pain. How can you be so chirpy? Don't you know that misery loves company? he didn't say. "I had a awful night's sleep—terrible headache—still have it."

"Oh, I'm sorry, pastor." She blinked. "You have your scheduled staff prayer meeting in half an hour. Do you want me to cancel it?"

If there's anything I need now it's prayer. "No. I'll tough it out," he replied in muted tones.

Susan studied his face for several seconds. He looked haggard. His hair was combed, but his right eye was bloodshot and tearing and partially closed apparently from sinus pressure. He wore the look of straining under a severe headache and maybe something even deeper. She grew concerned. "Can I get you something, pastor? Coffee? Aspirins?"

"I'll take both in my office as I prepare for the prayer meeting."

"I'll make a fresh pot of coffee and bring them in. Donut?"

Randy shrugged his shoulders then nodded. "Okay."

* * *

The internal stress was mounting. He could feel it in his heart and mind as well as his body. Emotionally he found himself dwelling on guilt. *Am I the cause of Sean's problem? Could I have discovered it sooner? What can I as his father do?* He was being tormented, and somehow he knew in his gut that this was far from over.

His appetite was waning and to him this was a sign of increasing anxiety. When he did eat, his stomach would gurgle and inflate with gas seeking to vent with noisy abandonment. To him they too were signs of acute acid indigestion, also from anxiety. Fatigue was rapidly become a familiar friend. He recognized that he yawned throughout the day, often just needing to take a fifteen minute 'power nap' to recharge his batteries before continuing his work.

The problem is that I have allowed my trust and faith in the Lord to fly out the window and that's when doubt, worry, and guilt walk in the door. Yes, I know this, but I feel powerless to fix it.

A knock at the door.

He walked and opened his door to let in Lester, Mike, and Rick, with Susan pulling up the rear with a tray of coffee cups and donuts in her hands. Susan walked to Randy and handed him two aspirins that he quickly swallowed with a slug of his coffee.

"Pastor okay?" Lester observed.

"Godzilla headache," he replied. "Woke up with it."

Lester watched him carefully as if trying to discern the cause. "We'll pray you through it," he said.

I can always rely on you to support me, Lester. I hope that holds true for the rest of my staff. "Well, men, let's have our coffee and donuts before we pray," Randy said. With that Susan excused herself and walked out.

With coffee in hand, Lester walked over to Randy's side, smiled, and pulled up a chair. "Everything okay, pastor? You look like you lost your best friend."

Randy shook his head. "I'm fine, Lester. Thanks."

The meaning was clear: *not now*! Lester's smile faded as he retreated back to his chair.

"Men, we need to come together and first of all, pray for our ministry here at Plantation Gate, then pray for each other's needs, then the congregation, and finally for our nation and community."

Mike studied Randy carefully and quickly recognized the routine prayer itinerary, but something was different with his pastor today. He couldn't nail it down, but knew something was troubling him apart from the headache. He picked up where Lester left off. "You look like the weight of the world is on your heart, pastor. Is there anything we can do for you? A special prayer request perhaps?" he solicited with deep kindness.

Randy tried feverishly to recover from his maudlin frame of mind but it was not meant to be. He looked intently at each one of his men in front of him. They were not only his fellow co-laborers in the Lord, but friends as well. His heart suddenly filled with a supernatural love for each of them, a love that transcended secret thoughts and holding back. Love changes everything, right? These men genuinely cared for him as their pastor. They were here to help him through his personal struggles and emergencies as he was for them. He needed help with his burden. It was too heavy to carry alone. "I have a family crisis at home and need to be surrounded with prayer," he began as his face contorted from the worry.

"Is it with Laurie? Tiffany? Sean?" Mike explored passionately.

"It's Sean," he said, shaking his head in dismay. "He—" he broke off and began to sob—"he's got a drug problem."

"Oh my God," Rick exclaimed as Lester buried his face in his hand.

"How bad?" Mike asked.

"He's on cocaine and oxycodone," he said dazedly.

Mike groaned. "Oh, no. What's his condition now?" Mike followed up caringly.

"He promised to get help, but he's playing games and hasn't gone yet," Randy explained.

Lester lifted his head and raised his hand. "We had a recent incident involving Sean and I suspected he was doing drugs."

"Who else knows?" Rick asked.

"Stephanie and Tiffany also know, but that's it," Randy added.

Rick and Mike nodded. "Laurie?" Rick asked.

Randy shook his head and wiped his tears. "I've kept it from her. I only told her he had a drinking problem. My thinking is that I can spare her this heartache. I believe he will get the help he needs—" he paused, "…and maybe she'll never have to know."

Mike didn't want to be the voice of reason, but he knew he had to advise his pastor with the real facts. "The problem with that course of action it that this whole thing could backfire in your face, pastor," he noted. "If anything goes wrong, Laurie will point to you and ask why you didn't tell her the truth."

Silence.

Frustration.

"I feel compelled to wait before telling her," Randy said after a moment of contemplation. "I'm waiting for the Lord to work things out."

"And what about the congregation? What if they start asking questions?" Mike asked with eyes pleading for understanding.

"Right now this is a family secret," Randy said, gathering composure. "I have brought you men into my family circle since you are my co-workers, friends, and confidants, but this is to remain within our confine here as of now." He drew a deep breath. "Do I have your promise that this will go no further?"

"What about our wives?" Mike asked respectfully.

"I'd rather that the wives be kept out of this for now," Randy replied. "We'll see how things go."

Lester raised his hand. "Pastor, I don't think Sean should be involved in the youth while this is in his life. He should stand down."

Randy nodded. "Absolutely. I'll take care of that." He turned to Mike. "Mike, look for a suitable substitute until we get this straightened out." He reached over to his desk to grab his bible for the devotion then added, "Again, do I have your promise?"

They all nodded. "Okay, now let's get on with the rest of our devotion and prayer meeting."

After the ten-minute devotion, Mike began the prayer time and spiritually transported the team to the very Throne Room of God to intercede on behalf of their pastor.

Randy was greatly refreshed.

* * *

Yes, this could be considered 'manipulation' or 'deception,' Randy thought, but he could not bring himself to tell Laurie the whole truth. He had to use whatever resources God made available to him without engaging the woman he loved and sought to protect. He thought about it in depth and could not wait any longer. He had to implement his plan to rescue his son.

"Where's Laurie?" Stephanie asked as she walked into Randy's office to see Tiffany fidgeting in one of the stuffed chairs.

"Hey, Stephanie," Tiffany said with a wave. She took the afternoon off from school to help her father during this crisis.

"Laurie's at a prayer luncheon at Sawgrass Heights Church," Randy replied. "God orchestrated this time for her to be out so we could meet to formulate my plan for Sean."

Tiffany glanced at the clock above Randy's door. "He's due here in five minutes," she said nervously.

Stephanie dropped into the other stuffed chair and closed her eyes. She had to pray and ask the Lord for wisdom and guidance, the kind that only comes from the Holy Spirit. "Okay, what is *your* plan, pastor?"

"In brief, either he submits to therapy now, or we advise the authorities of his addiction," Randy said dolefully. "Naturally that precludes his involvement with the youth here at the church."

"Is Mike, Rick, and Lester on board with the plan?" Stephanie asked curiously.

"Yes, I told them about Sean, and they are in agreement."

Tiffany turned to look into the parking lot. "He's here, dad," she said.

Randy picked up his desk phone and buzzed Susan. "Susan, Sean is on is way in. Please ask him to come to my office now."

Moments later he opened the door and scanned the room. "What's going on?" he asked in surprise. "Looks like some kind of tribunal."

"Come in and close the door, Sean," his father instructed. "We need to talk."

They all carefully inspected him with their eyes. He looked normal.

Randy motioned for him to drop off his backpack, find a seat and sit down. "Sean, we want to speak to you peaceable and clearly, so I want you to be quiet while we tell you why we want to see you." Randy stood up from his desk and walked in front of him. "I wanted to see you early in the morning while you were still lucid; before you started any funny business," he began succinctly. "We know just about everything there is to know about your drug addiction," he said while glancing at Stephanie and Tiffany. "Stephanie came to me so as not to violate Tiffy's pledge to you, but because of your last episode with George you have made it impossible to postpone any decisions for you to act on your own to get treatment. So don't think your sister betrayed you.

"We know about George and your cocaine, we know about your oxycodone from Canada, and we have a pretty good idea about how deeply you're involved in this habit." Sean squirmed in his chair and raised a hand to be heard. His father shook his finger in his face. "Just listen!" he snapped.

"Sean, right now you're a functioning addict," Stephanie argued. "But you will soon cross over to the other side where you will be totally incapacitated. I know what I'm talking about from all the years I have been involved in and out of the homeless life where many drug addicts wind up. And you can take it from me, your habit will only get worse. So don't lie to yourself and think you can stop this anytime you want—"

Tiffany cut in. "Sean, Satan has you right where he wants you. The world of drug addiction is from the pit of hell and there's no way around it. You need to come to grips with the fact that you're in deep and need help to climb out of the pit."

"Good advice," Randy approved.

"Tell me something, Sean," Stephanie probed. "South Florida is notorious for some pain management doctors prescribing recreational drugs along with other anesthetics to excessive proportions, so are you connected with any doctor? I believe your drug dependence requires more than we discovered."

"Alright! Alright!" he protested. "Guilty! So what do you want me to do? I'm really trying to get off these things." He gulped in a mouthful of air. "And what about you, Tiffany, have you come clean?" Then he turned to his father and pointed his finger at him. "If you weren't so consumed with your new building and this church and paid more attention to your family, maybe you could have helped me before things went this far!"

"Stop right there, Sean!" Randy argued, his headache pain climbing unchecked. "Don't play the blame game with me! You're deflecting and it doesn't work. You need to come to terms with your addiction and get help and that's what this is all about. Trying to pin your problems on somebody else doesn't work."

"Your father is right," Stephanie affirmed. "And my question remains. What other 'helpers' are you on?"

"COME CLEAN SEAN!" Tiffany shouted then burst into tears. "This secret of yours has been exposed by God and you must come clean now! God will not be mocked!"

Tiffany got to him. He couldn't stand to see her cry. "Don't cry sis," he said. "I'll get help, I promise."

With that he reached into a hidden pocket in his backpack and pulled out a plastic pocket coin container, opened it and placed three pills on Randy's desk.

Stephanie walked to the desk and examined them. "What are they?" she said, picking them up in her hand.

He joined her at Randy's desk and took one pill into his hand and said, "This is Adderall. I take this to help me in school. It helps me to stay focused." Then he held up another pill. "This is Alprazolam or Zanex. It helps me if I have a panic attack. Picking up the last pill, "This is Vicodin. This helps me when I'm in pain."

Tiffany shook her head in disgust. "This is terrible. You're on all these along with cocaine and oxy?"

Stephanie motioned for her to calm down as she nodded to Randy. "Sean," she began. "I hope I can appeal to your sense of reason. These prescription drugs are amphetamines and psychoactive drugs that bring about serious side affects when abused. These include altered mental states and depression along with many of the symptoms you are experiencing—the sweats, the loss of weight, the forgetfulness. Not to mention that cocaine intoxication can lead to suicide."

"Whoever this doctor is that is prescribing these should have his license to practice revoked!" Randy squawked.

"I'll go cold turkey!" Sean offered in defense. "I'll quit right now!"

"That doesn't work, Sean!" Randy said. "What you are going to do is to get into a drug rehab program under the guidance of a licensed Christian therapist and counselor." He stood up. "No discussion! Clear?"

Sean nodded in submission as he stared at Tiffany who appeared to be in anguish.

"I've arranged for you to see a colleague of mine in another church ministry who does Christian Counseling with a special attention to drug addiction," he instructed. "This requires you to make a commitment before God and us here that you will follow through with this."

"Does mom know?" Sean asked sheepishly.

"No. She does not know and we're trying to spare her the pain. For now this is our family secret," Randy allowed.

"Pastor Randy!" Stephanie exclaimed, "Look at Tiffany! She's—" she stood up, quickly sucking in air to catch her breath. "She's about to—" Tiffany suddenly ejected a large volume of vomit then grabbed her stomach, doubled up in the chair, then fell over on to the floor. "Oh my God!" Stephanie cried out and rushed to her side. "She's unconscious!"

"Sean, call an ambulance!" Randy shouted as he jumped to her side.

Sean grabbed his cell phone and called the operator, explained the emergency demanding an ambulance be sent to the church, then joined them at Tiffany's side. "I'm sorry, Tiffy!" he cried out as the color drained from his face. "I'm sorry."

"O, Lord, help us in yet another crisis," Stephanie cried out, beseeching God for mercy on this family. As she opened her eyes she saw Laurie's car pulling into the parking lot. "Pastor Randy!" she yelled out. "Laurie just pulled into the church yard. You had better go to her before the ambulance pulls up and scares her. We are here with Tiffany. Go, hurry!"

With his heart pounding, Randy went to meet Laurie with no clue as to what happened. As he stepped outside he could hear the wail of the ambulance approaching.

* * *

NINE

Susan and Stephanie shook their heads in anguish as they looked at Randy and Laurie holding each other as they watched their daughter being wheeled out of the church in a gurney and placed in an ambulance. "Can I drive you to the hospital, pastor?" Stephanie asked.

"No," Randy replied through tears. "We'll follow behind the ambulance." He turned to Sean who sat in the corner of the room with his head in his lap, crying. "Sean, pull yourself together and come with us to the hospital. Your sister is going to need you."

Sean slowly lifted his head and nodded mechanically at his father. "Okay," he said, wiping away his tears with his shirtsleeve.

* * *

Laurie distracted herself from the crisis by concentrating on her wristwatch as they traveled the distance of some nine miles to Plantation General, but it seemed to be an interminable period of time to travel while navigating the heavy traffic. "What's going on?" Laurie asked. "Has Tiffy been sick and we didn't notice?"

Randy didn't reply, being lost in his own search for answers. They all just hung their heads in sadness the rest of the trip.

* * *

Sean rebounded and scooted ahead of his parents into the ER as they went directly to the receptionist counter. "That's my sister the paramedics are wheeling in!" he exclaimed. "Can we go inside with them?"

The receptionist waved him off. "Absolutely not," she said resolutely. "When the duty ER nurse comes out and says it's okay, then you can go in." She handed him a clipboard as Randy and Laurie appeared behind him and added, "Please fill this out and return it to me."

Randy took a deep breath and started toward the waiting room when he suddenly turned to Laurie and said, "Wait a minute! I'm a pastor and I can go with Tiffy right now." He put his arm around her and said, "You wait here with Sean and complete the intake form and when it's okay I'll come and get you." Seconds later he walked off as Stephanie walked in the ER from the parking lot.

When Randy saw Tiffany his stomach erupted with the dry heaves. He had never seen his daughter in such a condition. He could see that she was semi-conscious and straining for relief from the pain while in a fetal position, attempting to free her body of the relentless agony. Her vomit had dried on her lips, cheeks, and blouse as a vivid reminder of her critical condition.

"Pastor Randy," a nurse said as she pulled the privacy curtain aside and walked into the cubicle, "we'll take care of your daughter. Don't you worry about her."

Randy assumed the word got out quickly who he was and why he was here. "Has the doctor seen her yet?" he asked.

"Not yet," she replied with a smile. "He's working his way down here. We have an influenza epidemic on our hands and many of our senior citizens have been stricken with it." She touched him on his shoulder. "In the meantime we're going to run some tests."

Randy watched the nurse hook his daughter up to a vital sign monitor then slip a thermometer clip on her finger before starting an IV saline solution. Moments later she drew three vials of blood then applied the EKG probes. He looked up at the aging nurse who apparently had enough experience to give him a word of encouragement. "Your daughter has a good heart rate," she said after glancing at the EKG. "Strong heart too."

Randy looked up at the monitor as it recorded her vital signs and forced a smile. "Praise the Lord," he said numbly then looked at the nurses ID badge. "Thanks Shirley," he said dolefully. Shirley smiled and closed the privacy curtain as she walked out to the nurse's station.

He sat down in the only chair in the cubicle then shook his head before squeezing his eyes shut. "Lord, help," he groaned and started to fill up with tears. Moments later someone opened the privacy curtain once again.

"Pastor Randy, I'm Doctor Percy," the man announced as he walked in with Shirley. He shook

Randy's hand and then walked to Tiffany's bed. "Now, let's see what's going on with you young lady," he said as he checked her vitals then motioned for Shirley to lift up the sheet to examine her.

Randy took a deep breath and shot a prayer up to the Lord as he stood up and carefully watched Doctor Percy perform his examination. *Lord, help us.* He clenched his fists as the doctor probed Tiffany's abdominal and pelvic area then turned aside and whispered, "Lord, even now we need you."

Tiffany moaned then shook her head!

"Well, looks like we woke our young lady up," Doctor Percy said to Shirley. Shirley nodded then replaced the cover sheet over Tiffany as she began to rally.

Randy went to her side and said, "I'm right here, Tiffy." She blinked several times to acknowledge him then closed her eyes and faded back into sleep.

Doctor Percy turned to Randy and asked, "Has your daughter had any problems with her period? Backaches? Urinary frequency or retention—abdominal discomfort or bloating?"

He looked at this doctor in amazement. As a medical professional in his late 40s he obviously was well qualified to make a diagnosis, but to ask her father these personal questions put Randy off. He shrugged his shoulders and said, "Her mother is in the ER waiting room. Can I get her?" Both Doctor Percy and Shirley nodded.

Dr. Percy took hold of Randy's hand. "Your daughter will be okay. I suspect this could be a uterine fibroid, but we will wait the outcome of the testing."

Randy's heart leaped within him. That didn't sound too serious, or so he thought. "Thank you doctor for that!" His eyes filled with tears. "God bless you," he said and marched off to the waiting room. Moments later he returned with Laurie.

Laurie walked to the doctor and said with a quiver, "My husband said you think it's a uterine fibroid? Should I be relieved? What's that all about?"

Dr. Percy escorted her over to the only chair in the cubicle and motioned for her to sit down. "I need to rule out certain things," he began, "so help me out."

"Of course."

"Well, I examined your daughter and see that she has been sexually active for some time now. At first I thought pregnancy might be an issue, but she is not pregnant. Next, as I asked your husband, has she had problems with her period? Has there been any urinary frequency or retention or backaches? Bloating?"

Laurie shot a look at Randy who overheard the doctor's remarks and stepped frantically to join them. The thought that their daughter has been sexually active caught them by total surprise. That there could be a hint of pregnancy really troubled them. *Do we really know our own daughter?* Laurie asked herself. No, they didn't really know her and any secrets she may be harboring.

Laurie rubbed her hands together in frustration and shook her head. "Not sure. I haven't really noticed any of those symptoms and I guess you could call me an ostrich with my head in the sand because I didn't know she was sexually active."

Randy looked at Dr. Percy. His shoulders rose and fell. "I'm at a loss. Really."

Dr. Percy glanced at Randy then patted Laurie's hand. "Don't take this news personal. It's very common among young men and women today to be sexually active and keep it from their parents. Believe me, you're not alone. I had to deal with my own daughter in the same manner."

Laurie felt a kindred spirit with the doctor amidst the disconcerting news. "If it is a uterine fibroid, Doctor Percy, what happens next?"

Dr. Percy looked over at Tiffany and answered, "A uterine fibroid is a benign tumor that originates from the smooth muscle layer of the uterus. Typically these tumors are found in females during the middle and later reproductive years and while asymptomatic, they can grow and cause heavy and painful menstruation and painful sexual intercourse along with urinary frequency and urgency. They can be either single or multiple." He paused and added while pointing, "You folks wait in the waiting room while we run some more tests, in particular, a gynecologic ultrasonography and an MRI."

Laurie nodded then grabbed Randy's hand and walked with him out to the waiting room. Moments later Shirley walked into Tiffany's cubicle and wheeled her up to radiology for testing.

* * *

Randy sat next to Laurie and studied her carefully as Stephanie and Sean looked on. Her maudlin frame of mind disturbed him. He knew her well and was troubled in his spirit. She was somehow blaming herself for Tiffany's crisis. He also sensed she was feeling guilty.

Laurie focused on a small crack in the floor tile of the ER room allowing her mind to fill with negative thoughts. She shut the rest of the room out. Despite her spiritual upbringing she could not shake the feelings that only culminated in sorrow and despair. *How come I didn't have enough discernment to know what was going on in my own home? How come I didn't realize my daughter was having sex with her boyfriend? Am I so filled with self that I'm blinded to my children? Lord, have I failed you in leading my children to know you and your word? Have I deliberately looked the other way— not wanting conflict?*

She glanced at Randy. *How come he didn't see this coming? He's the spiritual head of our family—our pastor—how come he didn't watch out for his family? Is the church more important than us? How could our daughter have changed so much without our noticing? Her value system that I thought was so strong in Jesus has obviously shifted. The doctor did say she was having pre-marital sex for some time. This is not a one night slip-up. What happened Tiffy?* She shook her head in misery.

"Where are you?" Randy probed. He put his arm around her. "She'll be all right. Don't worry."

She looked into his eyes, exploring; begging for answers. "Yes, I believe the Lord will take care of her and she'll be okay, but to find out this way that she's been having sex with Alex for who knows how long now devastates me. I guess I expected more from my daughter. I did notice Tiffy was eating more and when I teased her she was hostile," she began to sob. "She hasn't been herself for weeks but I thought it was finals and the pressures of school. Now I realize she probably thought she was pregnant and was terrified as to what to do. The fact that she felt she couldn't talk to her mother proves I've failed. This is just unimaginable to me." Then she bit her lower lip and added as she motioned with her hand, "With me these things are always vertical—between God and me. Why does he allow these things to happen if we're serving him in ministry?"

Randy wanted to say words of comfort to Laurie. He wanted to give her answers that would make sense but he felt their whole world was upside down. Their family was in crisis and nothing made sense. His stomach suddenly knotted up. *Family secret? Oh my God! What will happen if she finds out about Sean?* He shot a prayer up to God. *Lord, I need wisdom, guidance and your grace! How can I explain her question that becomes an imponderable of God? Why does he allow his servants to suffer?* He pointed toward the vending machines. "Can I get you something?"

"No," Laurie replied with suffering eyes.

Randy gestured to Stephanie and Sean. Stephanie shook her head. Sean nodded and walked with his father to the coffee maker. "Mom doesn't look so good," he began. "What did the doctor say?"

Randy poured himself a cup of coffee. "He said he believes she has a uterine fibroid tumor. He's taking tests to confirm his preliminary diagnosis."

"Is that serious?"

"Probably not, but will undoubtedly require surgery to remove it."

Sean scratched his head. "So why is mom so…" he looked over at her as she continued to pat her eyes with her handkerchief. "…so upset? I would think that she would be relieved."

He turned and stared into his son's eyes. "Because she learned today about the secret that Tiffany's been having sex with Alex. It is going to be some time before she processes that revelation."

Sean returned the stare as the color drained from his face. "What about me?"

Randy's breath caught in his throat and he gave his son a lethal glance. "It will destroy her."

Sean put his hand to his mouth as he registered the look on his father's face. The realization of the potential damage to his family from secrets was quickly coming into view.

* * *

Stephanie jumped to her feet as Dr. Percy approached them. "Pastor Randy!" she exclaimed, "the doctor."

Randy quickly woke from his power nap, flashed his eyes at the doctor and turned to find that Laurie was now at the coffee machine. She bolted to his side.

"Good news," Dr. Percy began. "The MRI confirmed the presence of the uterine fibroid so we have her being prepped for a non-invasive intervention that does not require an incision. We will use the Magnetic Resonance guided Focused Ultrasound (MRgFUS) to destroy the tumor."

Randy took a deep breath and forced a smile as he turned to Laurie. "Okay," he said. "What next?"

"The procedure takes about one to three hours depending on the size of the fibroids and we can expect a full recovery," Dr. Percy explained. "So you might want to go out and get yourselves something to eat and come back in a few hours." He smiled and placed his hand on Laurie's shoulder. "Rest assured, mom, we will take good care of your daughter."

Randy's heart reveled in Dr. Percy's encouraging report. "Thanks doc. We're trusting the Lord to work through you."

Dr. Percy grinned as he pointed up and said, "With His help, we cannot fail."

* * *

Randy walked out of the ER waiting room into the hospital parking lot then pulled out his cell phone and pressed the speed dial number for Alex Sanders. As he meandered to a remote area of the lot he signaled Laurie and Sean to escort Stephanie to their car while he made the call.

Seconds later Alex answered, "Mr. Bradshaw!" he exclaimed. "I just found out that Tiffany was taken to the hospital—I'm on my way there now." He gulped in fresh air and added, "Is she all right?"

"She's undergoing surgery for a uterine fibroid tumor and will be under for several hours," Randy explained with a tone that conveyed impatience. "We'll be back after we've had something to eat. Can you wait for us?"

"Of course," Alex replied. "I'll see you later."

Randy nodded then ended the call and suddenly realized he was grinding his teeth unwittingly. He took a deep breath and walked toward his car. *I'll deal with you later.*

"Who was that you were on the phone with?" Laurie asked once he sat in the car.

"Alex," Randy replied in a muted tone.

"What did he say?"

"He found out about Tiffy and is on his way here," Randy said. Then he bit his lip. "I plan to have a 'little' talk with him when we return from the restaurant."

Laurie shook her head then lowered her visor mirror to see Sean and Stephanie conversing in the back seat then reminded herself not to vent her anger in mixed company. "I want to be in on your 'little' talk with Alex," she said.

Randy's finger hung suspended over the ignition button as he turned to Laurie and saw the fury in her eyes. "He's got a lot to account for," he said then started the engine.

* * *

Randy's eyes locked on Alex at the coffee machine the very second he returned to the waiting zone of the ER. The pizza Randy gulped down at the restaurant started to back up from his stomach, letting him know that his acid reflux problem would now reach its zenith once he confronted Tiffany's lover. A title he despised.

Laurie snuffled several times to signal her newly acquired disapproval of Alex then walked slowly behind Randy to Alex's side while Sean and Stephanie grabbed magazines off the rack and sat down.

"Mr. Bradshaw," Alex began excitedly as he glanced at his wristwatch, "I just spoke with the nurse and she said that Tiffany is still in surgery. Maybe another hour, then she'll be in recovery."

Randy dismissed the news as redundant and replied gruffly. "We've had a tough time with this business, Alex, and we need to talk," He motioned for him to follow the both of them to a quiet area of the ER. Laurie lagged behind and noticed Alex's hands were shaking as he walked as if he were expecting a scolding.

Randy cleared his throat then pointed toward the OR ward and said, "While our Tiffany is undergoing surgery I want you to know that we are very upset and offended that you have been having sex with her."

Alex flushed and his eyes widened as he flashed a look at Laurie. "Mr. Bradshaw—"

Randy cut him off. "There's no point in denying it, Alex. The doctor examined Tiffany and then shocked us by telling us she is not a virgin and has been having sex for some time now."

"How could you have stolen our daughter's virginity?" Laurie said with a wounded look on her face and her voice vibrating with intensity. "With your parents being missionaries, we expected more from you. We would have expected you to observe a pledge of purity until you two got married." Laurie patted the tears streaming down her face then walked off.

"Mr. Bradshaw, I'm sorry you had to find out this way," Alex said in contrition, "but I love your daughter and want to marry her."

"That's all well and good, and if that happens—so be it," he exclaimed. "But for now, I can't see God's blessing on your lives. You both know the word of God and you profess to believe it. Why would you think you can violate God's word without consequences?"

"I don't see the Lord that way," Alex said discordantly. "I see the Lord as a gracious God, not One of vengeance for what you call our wrongdoing. If we love each other and plan to get married, doesn't that make it right?"

"No, it doesn't make it right," Randy argued. "If indeed it was right, then every couple that is living together today can justify their behavior before God by claiming, 'we love each other and we *are* going to get married.' But what they don't say is '*someday*.' And that '*someday*' may be five years down the line. So in my mind it's nothing more than fornication."

Alex would not win today with any form of justification and he knew it. "I'm sorry," he said with pleading eyes. Randy turned and walked over to join the others.

Moments later Dr. Percy entered the room in his scrub suit and walked to Randy and Laurie. "Tiffany is out of surgery and is in recovery." He smiled and added, "We already did a biopsy and everything looks good. She should be coming out of anesthesia in half an hour or so. She will be able to go home in two days."

Laurie's breath caught in her throat. "Thank you Lord!" she said aloud then hugged the doctor.

He in turn nodded and said to Randy, "May God bless you and your family."

Sean rushed to their side and said, "What did he say. Is Tiffy okay?"

Randy put his arms around them both, closed his eyes and shot a short praise to God. "He said 'everything looked fine.'" He waved to Stephanie to join them then glanced over at Alex who sat alone. *Good.*

* * *

Examine yourself, his spirit demanded. Randy paused momentarily as they walked through their front door and questioned this word from his conscience.

Laurie stopped short behind him. "What is it?"

"Oh, nothing," he said with a shake of his head trying to dismiss the thought.

Laurie shrugged her shoulders. "Sean and I will put the dinner on," she said and waved to Sean to assist her in the kitchen.

Randy walked slowly into their screened-in patio and sat down. Seconds later the thought ran through his mind again: *Examine yourself.* He swallowed hard. *Lord, is your Spirit nudging me?* He shook his head trying to shake loose the nagging thought. *Test me, O LORD, and try me, Examine my heart and my mind.* "Yeah, Lord," he whispered to himself, "I've preached on that text many times." The Lord was not going to let it go today.

He suddenly remembered that tomorrow was Plantation Gate's communion service and he would be reminding the congregation that before they could participate in the monthly observance of the Lord's Supper, they had to go before the Lord and review their heart, conscience, motives, and future plans to see if there were any obstacles to worship. *Transparency.* "Yeah, Lord, I know that I must be *transparent* as a pastor, husband, and father," he reminded himself just above a whisper. He stood up and stared into the kitchen at Laurie then contemplated his next move. *What to do?* He sat back down again in helpless frustration.

Lord, he mused, *I don't have it in me to be totally transparent with her. If I am, it will destroy our family. She isn't ready to learn all about Sean. After seeing how she reacted to Tiffy having sex with Alex—it will destroy our family. I just can't do it now.*

Examination. Transparency. The words began to circulate in his mind. He couldn't rid himself of them. They would haunt him for several days until he occupied his mind with other things thus overpowering his spirit and conscience. Relief came, but the dismissal displeased the Lord.

"Dad, dinner's ready," he heard, shattering his meditation. He followed Sean into the kitchen.

* * *

Randy armed the security system then turned off all the house lights and walked to his bedroom. He hesitated at Sean's bedroom door. No music. No lights. No nothing. Quiet. *Praise the Lord,* he thought, the monster from the ID is dormant tonight.

As he opened his bedroom door he saw Laurie dressed for bed but sitting in a chair. She looked like she was staring into space. *Oh, Lord, give me words to comfort my wife. Keep me strong and relying on you.* "Laurie, honey, come to bed. It's been a long, hard day."

"Randy, I don't know what to say to her. I'm so disappointed and just a little bit angry."

"I know sweetheart," he said softly, "but Tiffy has to settle this with the Lord and we have to be here for her to encourage and reconcile her back to God. She doesn't need us to judge her."

"You know how much I love our little girl—I'm hurting for her and the decision she might regret. Okay, so the best place to leave it is with our Father in heaven."

He reached for her. "Let me hold you in my arms until you fall asleep."

* * *

TEN

The rapturous music from Borodin's *Polovtsian Dance* from Prince Igor filled the cabin of his car as he drove to the church. *I love classical music. It soothes my spirit.* But the nudging from God continued. *Transparency.* He switched the tuner on his satellite radio from Classical to Christian as *Casting Crowns* sang *Somewhere in the Middle.* After listening to the lyrics for two minutes: "That's where I'm at," he said to himself as he looked at his eyes in the rearview mirror. "Firmly entrenched in midair."

A surge of guilt swept over him like a tidal wave. *Check your motive, man. The Spirit is prompting you and your staff thinks you should tell your wife and the congregation. If Laurie finds out about Sean and your involvement, she will be adamant in her feelings of betrayal.* A voice from within whispered a warning to him: *Your ministry and marriage are headed for deep waters unless you become transparent. Trust the Lord in all your ways.* "But it's just too much right now for me to handle," he said aloud to himself. "I'll do the right thing at the right time." He fought the negative thoughts off by rehearsing his favorite Bible memory verses.

Soon he was at the church.

* * *

"Mike Rice came in early to see you," Susan announced as Randy walked by her. "He's waiting outside your office." She smiled and added with a slight giggle, "He brought you a coffee and donut."

"The way to a man's heart is through his stomach. Isn't that an old saying?"

Susan nodded in affirmation. "I've heard that before!"

On second thought, I hope it isn't a peace offering, he didn't say. An unscheduled meeting by a staff member on a Thursday gave him cause for alarm. It usually spelled trouble.

* * *

"Good morning, Randy!" Mike said briskly as he stood up with coffee cup in hand. "Thought we would start the morning together with a shot of caffeine."

"Great!" Randy replied and showed him into his office.

Mike placed the donut along with an envelope on Randy's desk then took a seat.

Randy reached for the donut as Mike said, "Suzy and I wanted to send a get-well card to Tiffany, so I thought I would ask you to deliver it to her."

"Very thoughtful," Randy replied.

"Pastor Randy," Mike began slowly, "I wanted to take the opportunity to talk to you, brother-to-brother, if that's all right with you."

Randy sat down at his desk and began to nibble on the donut while at the same time demanding of himself to remain calm—no matter what happened today.

"Suzy and I really believe you are a man of God and that you want to honor the Lord in our church, your family, and your life," he continued. "And it's because we love our church and your family that we're praying for you every day. So we would like to know if there is anything in particular that we should pray for?"

Randy swallowed a gulp of coffee. "Admittedly, we do need prayer."

Mike ratcheted up his request. "I know what's going on with Sean, and now Tiffany and am wondering if there is any—"

"—unconfessed sin in my life? My family?" Randy blurted out to finish Mike's sentence. "Some dark secret in our family that is now being exposed?"

"Pastor Randy, please don't take this the wrong way," he half apologized and argued, "but as your assistant pastor I need to know how to pray for our church and your family."

"I know, I know, Mike," Randy said humbly. "And I want to receive your questions in the right spirit, so please understand that our family is undergoing severe testing and we solicit your prayers, but the Lord is still writing the script and frankly, I really don't know what He's doing in my family." He shook his head slowly, then: "I'm in a desert experience, but not in sin, and I don't believe my Laurie is either. As far as Tiffany and Sean is concerned, that's a different matter, but I don't think this crisis is related to their spiritual condition no more than when Christ was asked about the man born blind; who committed the sin? himself or his parents? Christ profoundly responded, neither, but that the blindness was for the glory of God. Remember, my family is not immune from social problems and addictions that have taken America captive."

Mike nodded. It seemed right. It seemed logical. But only God would sort that one out. It was not for him to challenge him on that point any further. He squirmed in his seat as if to muster up the courage to ask the next question. "We need to know about Sean since he is an important part of our church leadership. Somehow Sean got on the wrong path and we want to help him in whatever way we can. He has been a valuable part of the ministry and the youth look up to him. Although we have all agreed to have him step down from serving in this capacity, how can we guide him back to Jesus, his first love?"

Randy sighed deeply. "I appreciate that. I can only tell you that he made a profession of faith at youth camp ten years ago and there were signs that this was a genuine salvation experience." He paused to reflect then added, "Just love on him and let's wait on the Lord to work things out."

Mike nodded approvingly. "You have often taught on the fruit of regeneration that meant when one is converted the Holy Spirit gives them a passion for the Word of God, a passion for the lost, and a changed life. Are you doubting this in connection with Sean?"

Randy bit his lower lip, not realizing a tear formed in his right eye. "Not sure," he answered. "Not sure." He temporized then: "We raised him in a godly household and tried to be a godly example to him." He shrugged his shoulders and repeated his reply, "Not sure."

Mike recognized the signs of stress in his pastor's face and voice. He had to be a helper, not a hinderer. "What can Suzy and I do to help?"

Randy moaned with resignation. "Just pray for me and my family and Sean's counseling."

Mike stood up. "Sean's going to counseling?"

Randy nodded. "You're the only one I've shared that with. I demanded he get counseling outside of our church family."

"Hopefully that will bear some good fruit," Mike replied.

"We're praying the counseling will give us some telltale signs as to the underlying reason that Sean would turn to drugs," Randy added in somber tones. "From there we'll make decision as to his involvement in ministry."

"May it be so," Mike said with a smile and walked out feeling somewhat discouraged. He wanted desperately to hear that his pastor had received from God a godly solution to his family's problems. *Has he discussed the problems with Laurie? Who am I to tell another man much less my pastor how to run his family but I see disaster ahead because of his refusal to include his wife and church in this trial. Lord, I know Pastor Randy can't carry this load alone. Please help him.*

* * *

Lester knocked on Randy's office door then stuck his head in to the room. "The deacons and staff are ready to pray over you before you give the message, Pastor," he said. As the senior deacon, Lester saw to it that the protocol for Sunday worship service was strictly observed. That meant he supervised the activities on behalf of his pastor who trusted him implicitly with the task.

"Thanks, Lester. Bring them in," Randy replied with a wave of the hand and then tucked his sermon outline into his Bible then closed it. Lester, Mike, Rick, and the other deacons promptly marched in and stood just inside the door. Randy nodded to Lester who then led them over to his desk and laid hands on him. They called upon God's Spirit to anoint their pastor and give him the words to both edify and challenge the congregation. Believing God, they embraced their pastor and walked out.

Moments later Randy joined the congregation in the sanctuary. After the worship team led the music and Lester gave the announcements, Randy ascended the pulpit.

* * *

Randy took particular notice of Laurie and Stephanie's faces as he opened up his Bible to his sermon text. Laurie was his most severe critic, with Stephanie being a close second. If his sermons received a passing grade from them, he believed he had connected with God and that the rest of the congregation would have felt the same. By reading their faces in advance he calculated whether or not he had a chance at success. *They were smiling! Hooray, I'm in!*

"Please open your Bibles to Philippians chapter four, verse nineteen," he began. He cleared his throat then quoted in a clear emphatic voice, "'And my God will meet all your needs according to his glorious riches in Christ Jesus.' Now what does that mean to you?" He pointed at the congregation, waving his finger horizontally. "Do you really believe Jesus will meet *all* your needs or just *some* of your needs?" He stepped away from the pulpit and stared into the crowd, pointing as before. "Is this simply a *suggestion* from the apostle Paul speaking for God, or is this a *promise* that we can rely upon?"

A thought flashed into his head: *Do you really believe this Randy? God has not met the needs of your family. Look at Sean. Look at Tiffany! You're a hypocrite!* He suddenly faltered and his mind went blank. He froze in place searching for his next word.

Oh, no!, Laurie thought as she held her breath then glanced at Stephanie and Sean. *He's in trouble.* She closed her eyes and quickly prayed for him while Stephanie blinked and Sean shook his head.

Randy stepped back to the pulpit then scanned his outline and continued, only an octave lower, "There are those who look at this as a *suggestion*, thinking that they can help God out when it comes to their needs, but they really believe that they are the principle providers, while the Lord is just a 'back-up.' They don't really trust the Lord to provide for them. They are not willing to wait for the Lord to supply for them, so they take matters into their own hands and go out and get what they need, despite the fact that they are unsure if this is the will of God. This can bring serious consequences.

"Then there are others who see this as a *promise*, but they corrupt the text and add, 'wants' instead of 'needs' and this can lead to a 'Santa Clause' mentality that believes our God will give you whatever you want—just name it and claim it!" He paused and shot a look at Laurie. *I'm okay*, he said with his eyes.

"I remember being at a weekly church prayer meeting many years ago," he continued, "and there was a man who was a senior citizen who years earlier was a medical student studying to be a doctor. One day he went into the nearby town and was attacked by two thugs who hit him over the head with a baseball bat and robbed him. He suffered permanent brain damage. Fast-forward many years to the prayer meeting. When it was his turn to make his request, he prayed that God would give him a car so he could travel from the nursing home to the church.

"Now I know that God could not possible answer that prayer! The man didn't even have a driver's license, much less the ability to manage an automobile." He slammed his hand down on the pulpit. "This was a *'want'* not a *need!* And many of you are in the same situation. You are praying for something—be it a new husband—a new home—a new job—whatever, and God is saying, 'this is a *want*, not a *need*!" He paused. "Are we on the same page?"

Several 'Amens' were voiced.

"Jesus made a profound statement in his Sermon on the Mount when he declared that we should not be anxious for our care or provision and that our God will supply all your needs. If he cares for the lilies of the field and the birds of the air—will he not take care of you—who are much more valuable?

"But here is the conditions in order for God to provide your needs, and you should listen carefully." He stepped away from the pulpit and walked to the staircase leading to the stage and then descended to the second stair and stopped. The pause had a mesmerizing affect on the congregation; there was not a sound to be heard. With his voice vibrating with intensity he bellowed out, "You must be born-again and have a relationship with Jesus Christ! If you are unsaved, you are on your own. That means you do not belong to Christ and because you belong to the world, you must fend for yourself!" *For several more minutes he continued in that theme, dramatizing the ineptitude and emptiness of a person fending for him or herself.*

Then: He grinned at the congregation and then raised one hand with his index finger extended. "Now some will say, 'I've been fending for myself so far, pastor, and I'm happy with where I'm at.' But let me remind you that your resources are just temporal, but Christ's resources are eternal. Yes, you may have financial security with a wonderful career, but in a moment, your business could fail or your health can turn and you could lose all of that overnight. But when we belong to Christ, he takes care of us. If we should lose our financial security, his promise is that he will replace it with something far better." He returned to the pulpit and added, "This is why David wrote in Psalms, 'I have been young and now I am old; yet I have not seen the righteous forsaken or his seed begging bread.' So why take a chance? If you're not sure where you stand with God, come forward now so that I can pray with you." He paused and nodded to Lester who took the cue. "Lester will be up here with me, so don't put it off any longer. Come forward now and get right with Jesus as we sing our invitation hymn." With that Rick Kelly and his wife sang, *Just As I Am.*

Four repeat visitors came forward along with one member for prayer. To Randy, it was a fruitful, rewarding worship service.

* * *

"What was going on when you suddenly paused while you were preaching?" Laurie asked once they were alone after the worship service.

He rubbed his chin and pondered the question. "Thoughts jumped into my mind from the *other side*! Satan was working my head and I was overwhelmed with thoughts that I'm not qualified to preach because our family is in trouble; that I'm a hypocrite. But in my heart I claimed the blood of Jesus and the accusations left me."

Laurie shook her head. "That was a fine sermon and you delivered it with power. No doubt Satan sent a spirit of confusion to try to trip you up so that people didn't hear it." She walked up to him and hugged him. "From now on I will pray for you while you preach," she promised.

Randy smiled, his eyes admiring her. "I'll treat you to lunch."

"Deal."

* * *

Today is going to be a good day, Randy reminded himself. *With Tiffy coming home today we'll be a family again.* He rebuked any negative thoughts surrounding Sean and resolved to set them aside. He deliberately suppressed the notion that Sean's drug problem was a widening hole in his family's spiritual umbrella that had been protecting them from the fiery darts of Satan. But ignoring the godly principle didn't make it go away. He knew inwardly that the day would come when he would have to deal with it. But today was not that day.

"Pastor Randy," Susan said, tapping lightly on his door. "Philip Van Fleming is on the phone."

A muscled jerked in his left cheek. *Ugh,* he thought. He shook his head. *Don't ruin my day Van Fleming.* While many viewed Van Fleming as a strong supporter of Plantation Gate Church, there were an equal amount of congregants who believed his support came in the form of dollars. The opponents believed those dollars influenced decision-making and promoted favoritism. Randy knew about the sentiments but still believed that there was redemptive value in his contributions provided they were allocated toward kingdom building. As far as favoritism was concerned, he was able to manage Van Fleming without him really knowing it. Or so he thought.

"Philip," Randy began, putting him on speakerphone and walking around his desk, "what is God doing in your life?!"

"Good things. Always good things!"

"Wonderful. So, how can I help you this morning?"

"Well, pastor, Sandy and I were just talking about yesterday's sermon and thought we would have some fellowship with you over the phone."

Randy swallowed hard. Having Van Fleming's wife on a conference call gave him a cramp. The thought that they *discussed* his sermon meant only one thing from them: questions leading to problems. "Okay, go ahead," he said, tongue-in-cheek.

"Pastor, Philip and I pray that all is well with you and your family," Sandy began cordially.

"We're doing well, thank you," Randy replied.

"And Tiffany?"

"Tiffany is coming home today. We're very excited, praise God."

"Amen! Ministry business okay?" she added.

"Yes, God is blessing us here at Plantation Gate."

"We're glad," they both said in unison.

"Pastor, Sandy asked me a question after your sermon that I was personally unable to answer," Philip chimed in.

"What was that?"

"She asked me if we were building up the congregation with *our* sermons? After discussing it we are asking you if you think your sermon may have polarized the audience since it was—" he paused then added, "—to a degree, caustic?"

"Polarized? Caustic?" Randy asked in defense, his stomach tightening. "What does that mean?"

"Well, we agreed with your text and how God will provide all of our needs, but when you made statements like 'Santa Clause mentality' and the 'unsaved' will have to 'fend for themselves' we think that those terms alienate people. Then the part about 'conditions' seemed to ratchet up the sermon where people were made to feel uncomfortable."

The John Jowett quote, '*God does not comfort us to make us comfortable, but to make us comforters*' flew into his mind. "Well, Philip, I don't think my role is to make people feel *comfortable* but to challenge them to have a closer, committed walk with Christ."

"Yes, yes, pastor, we agree with that philosophy of ministry," he replied, lowering his voice, "but maybe you should lighten up somewhat—I mean after all, don't you want to see more results from your sermons? Taking yesterday for example. Not one visitor or anyone else came forward for a decision for membership or salvation. Maybe those *numbers* would be better if the message was *lighter*."

Ouch! That hurt! Randy thought. But his ministry experience dictated that any pastor worth his salt must not look at the immediate results of his preaching and teaching since his role was to plant seeds and allow the Lord to bring the fruit of his efforts in His time. "Well, I don't look for *numbers*, Philip. I just preach as the Lord directs." He rubbed his right temple. He could feel another tension headache coming on him on top of an upset stomach.

"We agree, pastor," Sandy said. "But I've been looking on the Internet at some real prosperous Christian ministries and read about their approach to the unchurched and one thing you can't deny is the success of their method in winning souls to the Lord."

"I've noted in many of the national church websites that they don't preach judgmental sermons and that their dogma looks at the Bible with a very up-to-date position," Philip added with a tinge of authority. "Instead of the preacher interpreting the Bible text, these churches allow the hearer to interpret the meaning of the text to fit their own situation." He paused. "We think it's a good idea. It has a very modern style to it."

"Oh, I agree it's modern, and I have done my homework," Randy replied aggressively. *Modern* was the buzzword for him. "*Postmodernism* is what it is really called. I researched the current trend in many Christian churches toward *Postmodernism* and I didn't like what I found. It rejects the notion of truth as fixed, universal, objective or absolute. Any claim to Biblical truth is met with suspicion and any texts that are not pleasing to the postmodern mind are rejected as oppressive, patriarchal, heterosexist, homophobic, or deformed by some political or ideological bias. Categories such as 'sin' are rejected as harmful to self-esteem. Right and wrong are discarded as out-of-date reminders of a difficult and oppressive past. Teachings such as acceptance without repentance and wholeness without redemption are common themes in the postmodern church. Preachers are tolerated as long as they stick to therapeutic messages of enhanced self-esteem, but are resisted whenever they inject divine authority or universal claims to truth in their sermons. Postmodernists discard morality, along with other basic foundations of culture. They consider them harsh and totalitarian. So repulsive is the notion of God's wrath that many churches and postmodern theologians have tried to deny it altogether. God has become our next-door neighbor and our great cosmic companion, rather than the holy God of the Bible. A congregant may not know or care if they are saved or lost, but they really feel better about themselves." He took a deep breath. "So you see Philip and Sandy, this would not work in our church."

The bile in his stomach reacted to the discussion. It felt like an acid pit. The joy of ministry seemed fleeing with the incursion of heretical doctrines and apostate teachers and their relentless quest to dominate Christendom. Ministry was becoming more and more convoluted as mankind raced toward the end of the age. Lawsuits against churches, pastors falling into sexual sins, the Bible being discredited as a fable, and on it went. But he realized that the greatest threat was from within. The corporate church seemed to be eating itself up. With the widening of doctrinal gaps and escalating ecumenism that blurred denominational lines to the point where if one believed in God, regardless of what the name of that god was, there was unity. To Randy it was apparent that Satan was concentrating on dividing the church as he saw his days of mastery on earth coming to an end. The target seemed to be on doctrine and it's application.

His discussion with Rick popped into his mind and his warning that Plantation Gate needed to guard itself against the 'isms' that have infiltrated into society as well as the church. He had to hold his ground. "Philip and Sandy, I must disagree with you on this," he said after a moment of contemplation. "I'm aware of the different views on how to build a 'prosperous' church as you put it, and I, along with the leadership of this church will not buy into it. It is not of God and this humanistic, seeker-friendly persuasion under the guise of postmodernism has grieved the heart of God because the call of the church is to be the Bride of Christ in all that name includes which is a call to worship, holiness, sacrifice, and evangelism—and separation from the world. Not to pander to man's touchy-touchy feelings or their comfort zones."

Philip cleared his throat and Sandy snuffled ever so lightly. "Humph," Philip voiced. "I see. Well, I just wanted you to know what our thoughts were on this, but you're the pastor and we bow to your position."

"I appreciate you both," Randy replied after clenching his teeth and resisting the urge to fidget. "You're both an important part of this ministry. Thanks for sharing your thoughts with me."

"See you next Sunday," they both said then Randy ended the call.

Whether or not the issue would take wings and fly into other member's homes of Plantation Gate church via the Van Fleming pipeline was something that Randy had no control over. If it did go viral, he would address it at that time.

* * *

His afternoon ride from the church to home was fraught with anxiety. *And I thought today was going to be a good day. Not so.* The sour tasting conversation with Van Fleming was still in his mouth and the recurrent worry of Sean and his problem just would not go away, despite the happiness he felt over Tiffany's homecoming. *Command yourself to put these things out of your mind*, he told himself. Concentrate on positive things. He searched his mind and couldn't think of any as he drove into his garage.

"Where's my little girl?" he exclaimed as he turned the corner into the kitchen. *Force yourself to be joyful!*

"She's in the sunroom watching the TV," Laurie said with a smile then returned to stirring a pot on the stove. "I'm making her some hot soup. I'm on a campaign to fatten her up with some healthy meals."

Randy crept toward their sunroom and peeked in to see Tiffany and Sean on the sofa sharing a bag of BBQ potato chips. "Now I know why mom's heating up soup for you, to offset the junk food," he said with a guffaw. Then he hurried over and kneeled down to give her a kiss.

Tiffany held up her fingers that were laden with potato chip fragments. "Need to overcome the *taste-free* hospital food, dad!"

He laughed then turned to Sean. "How's my boy?"

"Doing well, dad," he replied. Randy sensed he was clean, hoping this was the outworking from his counseling sessions.

Laurie brought in a bowl of hot soup and placed it on the coffee table that stood in front of the sofa. She snapped her fingers and said, "Hand over the *goodies*." Tiffany clutched the bag of chips to her chest in mock revolt then smiled and handed them to her mother.

"Can I get you something, Sean?" his mother asked.

Sean shook his head signaling with thumbs up, "I'm good."

As Randy looked on at this brief interchange of his family members, he praised God in his spirit for this moment where his family was all at peace with each other, having fun. *Lord, give me rest round about from all of my enemies.* He refused to rob Laurie of her joy and so decided not to share with her the call from Van Fleming

* * *

Randy's cell phone chimed out the hymn *Redeemed* as he sat at his desk. The caller ID read Mike Rice. He tapped *Answer* to hear: "Good afternoon, pastor. I'm here at Pat's Subs. Can I bring you back one?"

Randy shot a look at his desk clock, amazed that his stomach had not been growling. "Yeah, that would be great, Mike. Make mine a tuna salad on whole wheat with American cheese and tomatoes."

"Got it! See you in fifteen minutes," Mike said then ended the call.

Randy looked forward to talking to Mike as his sounding board about the Van Fleming call, knowing that he could rely upon him for godly counsel. The lunch would be secondary.

* * *

Mike stood momentarily at the entrance to the church fellowship hall watching Randy wash down a portable table to prepare for their lunch. "Ta-dah! Lunch has arrived," he announced.

"You will be blessed!" Randy replied in jest.

Moments after Randy gave thanks to God, Mike took a large bite of his sub then a gulp of cola to expedite the swallowing then said, "I didn't get a chance to see you yesterday since you left early to see Tiffany, but Suzy and I enjoyed Sunday's sermon. Really on point."

Randy nodded. "Obviously there are those who disagreed," he explained between bites. "I received a call from Van Fleming and his wife who believe the message was too offensive. In short they think I should go the way of 'felt needs' that in turn would build up our popularity and membership. He cited that there was no decisions for salvation or membership to support his claim."

Mike stopped chewing, and with his mouth half filled with food said sharply, "He should take his money and stick it where—" he stopped short then swallowed. "Sorry, pastor," he said apologetically. "I didn't mean to be critical. I just go crazy over this post-modernistic mentality that is running through America's churches."

"I feel the same way," Randy agreed. "I told him that we are not buying into the wave of postmodernism and all of its trappings here at Plantation Gate."

"And—?"

"And…I could tell that he didn't like my response. I suppose they thought we could compromise and neuter our sermons and teaching to accommodate society," Randy explained. "Hopefully that will squash any notion of infiltrating our philosophy of ministry with doctrines that we are opposed to."

Mike finished his lunch then added, "Do you expect any reprisals from Van Fleming?"

"I hope not," Randy replied. "If so, we will deal with it harshly."

Mike's emotions soared and his eyes began to tear as he looked at his pastor. *I respect this man!* "Good for you, pastor!" he said in support. "Suzy and I are behind you one-hundred percent."

"I appreciate that."

"How are things at home with Sean and Tiffany?" Mike asked.

"Tiffany is recovering well, and Sean is still in counseling," Randy allowed. "Keep us in prayer, Mike. We're not out of the woods yet."

"Did you tell Laurie about Sean yet?" Mike ventured casually.

Randy bit his lip and shook his head. "Not yet. I just can't bring myself to tell her about Sean now. There's so much going on with Tiffany and other things," he answered. "I'm afraid she is too fragile right now," he added dryly.

Mike nodded compassionately but thought otherwise. He couldn't bring himself to criticize or advise his pastor when he was down. But in his prayer time with Suzy they hoped that his pride or the potential fear of losing respect from the congregation was not the reason for refusing to tell Laurie. *How long can you keep this secret?* A Proverb popped into his mind: *Pride goes before destruction, and a haughty spirit before a fall. Yes Lord, I remember your warning, but please watch over our pastor and his family.* "We understand, Randy, and we are committed to pray for you until things work out."

Randy stood up. "Thanks for the lunch." Then he said with a wink, "You have cleanup."

When he returned to his office he was surprised to find Laurie sitting in his desk chair gazing out the window.

* * *

"What's up, babe?" he asked as he walked in. "I'm delighted to see you."

Laurie turned to him and said, "I had a chat with our daughter this morning, and we need to clear something up."

Randy checked her mood and sensed a problem. He walked to one of the chairs by the window and sat down. "What's that?"

Laurie stood up and walked toward one of his bookcases and leaned against it. "To begin with, I think her hospital stay brought her closer to the Lord because this morning after you left she wanted to talk about her and Alex. I think it was what you often call a *catharsis.*

She wanted to get something off her chest so she confided in me about their relationship."

Randy immediately went on guard and said, "How bad is this going to be?"

"No. No," she replied. "It is not all that bad."

"What could be good about our daughter fornicating?"

She walked toward him and pulled up another chair and sat down within reach. "She said that Alex told her about us finding out in the ER that she is not a virgin. She was very upset about it."

"Rightfully so," he commented. "She should be."

She put her hand on his shoulder and added, "Well, she admitted that it was her idea to have sex with Alex. Not his."

"You're serious?"

"He tried to talk her out of it. He wanted to wait until they were married but she objected saying it would be a long time before they were financially able to get married."

Randy clucked reprovingly. "He didn't try hard enough if you ask me." He shifted in his chair. "What's the good part?"

"Well, for one thing, it does speak to Alex's integrity. He did not suggest or push her into having sex with him. It came from Tiffy. The other good thing if you want to look at this from a positive perspective, is that Tiffy made a pledge in front of me that the would not have further sex with Alex until they were married."

"Thank you, Lord, " he said in praise.

"I think she realized this medical scare with the tumor was a wake up call from God to get her life right so that she could be blessed," Laurie postulated.

"So what do we do now? Forget the whole thing?" Randy asked trenchantly.

"No. We can't just forget about it. But we can trust the Lord that she has repented of her sin and will keep her pledge. As for Alex, I think you need to talk to him. In particular, you need to apologize for any accusations you made and tell him about Tiffy's pledge and ask him to honor that."

Randy squirmed in his seat and raised a hand and then nodded. "I agree, but there's one thing I need to know before I speak to him."

"What is that?"

His lips twitched, and he said, "How come she didn't tell me?"

Laurie stared at him in helpless frustration. "Because she loves you as her dad and did not want to hurt you or your ministry." A tear appeared in her left eye. "She said she couldn't help herself—she loves Alex and gave in to her emotions."

He sighed deeply then cried in his spirit: *Lord, how long wilt thou look on? Rescue my soul from their destructions, mine from the lions. The world is devouring my family, oh Lord. Help.* "Okay, I'll make things right with Alex."

Laurie hugged him. "We'll get through this, Randy. We need to stay strong in the Lord."

—let me hide myself for a little moment, until these indignations pass, he didn't say.

* * *

ELEVEN

The entranceway to the counseling center was bordered with bright red desert rose bushes that seemed to illuminate the path to the door. The rosy pathway engendered a happy feeling for those seeking godly advice on how to manage the issues in life that seemed so troublesome and apparently taking control of them.

Cassie waved to Sean as he walked into the waiting room and went to the counter to sign the registry. "Good morning Sean," she said with a luminous smile. "Dr. Prentiss will be with you shortly, he's just finishing up his first appointment."

Sean nodded to the matronly-like woman then signed in and glanced at this favorite painting on the wall as he sat down. There were only two chairs in the room with one magazine rack and an artificial plant in the corner. Dr. Prentiss believed it was overpowering and intimidating when a counselee saw too many chairs in a waiting room. He believed it conveyed the impression that there would be many persons at one given point who would be sitting in the room wondering what the other person's problem was and why they were there. His philosophy was simply to carefully schedule each appointment to avoid having more than two persons in the waiting room at one time.

The modest counseling office had bookshelves lining one wall and on the opposite wall were two large nature paintings with bible verses written in calligraphy nestled in the bottom of the scene. Sean liked the one with the soaring mountainscape with snow melt providing a waterfall emptying into a serene lake where several white tail deer were sipping the water. Towering pine trees bordered one edge of the picture providing scale to the magnificent mountains in the background. When he gazed at it he felt at peace.

Sean pulled out his phone and went to the calendar application and realized this was his third appointment with Dr. Prentiss. He marveled that after the initial intake appointment, he actually looked forward to talking with him. He recognized that the doctrine of confidentiality prohibited his counselor from discussing or revealing any information they addressed with anyone other than himself unless he provided written permission. Because of this rule, he felt safe. He could talk to him about his innermost feelings knowing that he would not be judged or exposed.

"Sean, I need your co-pay," Cassie said, breaking up his thoughts.

Sean nodded then pulled out $15 from his wallet then walked up to the office and placed it on the counter. Cassie handed him a receipt before he returned to his seat. He agreed with his father that he would pay a small share of the fee out of his own personal money as his way of demonstrating his commitment and investment in the counseling sessions. Dr. Prentiss agreed that this practice, along with the counselee being held accountable for their home assignments, produced good results from counseling.

* * *

Twenty-five minutes passed before Dr. Prentiss' door opened and his counseling patient walked out. Sean eyed the smiling middle-aged woman as she made her next appointment and wondered what could possibly be going wrong in her life that necessitated Bible counseling. *I guess at one time or another, we all need to speak to someone for advice,* he thought. "Dr. Prentiss will see you now, Sean," Cassie said.

Dr. Prentiss had a PhD. In Christian Counseling and received most of his clients from pastoral referrals in the surrounding communities. His approach to all kinds of conflicts was what became known in the counseling field as 'nouthetic' counseling. The term came from the Greek that meant, "confrontational." In layman's terms it simply referred to the counselor appropriating all responsibility for the client's response to conflict to the client himself or herself. How they reacted to a situation or person who initiated the conflict made all the difference when applying Biblical principles. Many were uncomfortable with this form of counseling since it required individuals to examine themselves rather than shift the responsibility of the conflict to someone else.

Historically a person would come to him for help after exhausting secular counsel since their approach depended on philosophical, societal, or, human reasoning, apart from Biblical resources.

"Good to see you once again, Sean," Dr. Prentiss said. "Have a good week?"

Sean nodded and replied, "My sister came home from the hospital so the family had a good week."

"And you?" he asked pointedly.

Sean paused before answering. He liked his counselor who had a very soft approach in getting to know you and showed that he really cared for his clients. Besides being very personable he seemed pastoral in his inquiries that did not lead to condemnation but to mediation; something that Sean believed would benefit him. But there was a side to him that was intrusive when it came to faults or bad habits. He seemed intolerant when there was a Biblical injunction that mandated obedience. Sean began to recognize that with each successive session, he was digging in more and more. "I guess you could say I had a *fair* week."

Dr. Prentiss projected the image of a 50ish man who had it all together. He was married to a good-looking woman with two children [their picture was conspicuously placed on his office book shelf] and he himself was the epitome of discipline with his trim figure, suit and tie, and a Van-dyke beard [He later admitted to a good workout at the gym three times per week]. Sean believed the most important element in his profile was that he really knew how to draw a person into his confidence and therefore allow the counselee to trust them implicitly.

With clipboard in hand, Dr. Prentiss walked to the chair opposite Sean and sat down. He wrote something down then asked, "How did you make out with your homework assignment?"

"I emailed it to you," Sean replied.

"I'll check it later," Dr. Prentiss replied. "Give me the highlights."

Sean squirmed in his chair then said, "I had a little trouble with the Bible passage you asked me to explain. I know where you're going with the part about 'my body is being a temple of the Holy Spirit,' and what that means to a person who does drugs." Sean disclosed to Dr. Prentiss his history of drug addiction at his second session. What he didn't reveal was how deep his dependence had become and the full array of drugs being used.

"Drug addiction is a one-way street, Sean. You should know that. My task is to show you how you can have the victory in Christ over this addiction before it's too late."

He didn't like the word *addiction*. It conjured up in his mind that he didn't have control over his habit when he believed he did. He hesitated fractionally then: "I've been clean since I've been coming here, doc. I'm really trying." He thought for a moment then added, "With God's help I'll stay clean."

"Because of the nature of this addiction and your family situation," Dr. Prentiss explained, "you can only have me as your accountability partner. This is not like AA where you can call a partner when you feel yourself slipping and they can help you out of it. Because of that I must add a requirement to our relationship. I insist that you call me every three days between sessions and talk with me." He looked intently at him. "Clear?"

"Clear."

"Now let's dig into your relationship with Christ and what your responsibility to stay clean really means," Dr. Prentiss said.

Sean shifted his body weight. *We're really ramping this up now, aren't we doc!* he didn't say.

For the next forty-five minutes they discussed what Sean would consider later to be the most crucial session of all.

* * *

Dr. Prentiss walked to his file cabinet and pulled out Sean's folder to transfer his notes from the clipboard. He stood at the cabinet and studied the file for over fifteen minutes then turned and looked toward the window. "Now here is a young man who says that he has a personal relationship with Christ, yet tells me in confidence that he is a heavy drug user." His soliloquy continued, "He tells me he battles with doubts about his salvation experience and *that* I believe, is what plunged him to wrong decision-making and ultimately wrong behavior. Our sessions reveal little fruit that should be apparent in the life of a Christian, yet he claims that he knows his sins are forgiven."

He updated the file from today's session then returned it to the cabinet and walked to a painting on his wall. It was a print of Thomas Kinkaid's *Prince of Peace* from 1980. Then his heart filled with thoughts about the late painter. "Here is a man known as the *Painter of Light* who made a profession of faith back in 1980, attended a Bible-believing church, The Church of the Nazarene, yet died of acute intoxication from alcohol and Valium at age 54." He looked up. "How can a man with such a gift lose his way and stumble so greatly? What happened to him, Lord that he painted light but lived in darkness dependent on alcohol and drugs? What about the prodigal Son? Was he saved when he went off to riotous living or was the mercy and grace of His Father a picture of God's calling to our failures, assuring us that failure is never final with our Lord? Is Sean really saved?" He ended his soliloquy with the affirmation that he would have to go before the Lord and ask for a greater portion of wisdom to be able to counsel Sean more effectively.

* * *

Randy recognized Alex's car in his driveway as he turned the corner into his cul-de-sac. *Raw meat and gunpowder, right,* he said to himself. He would have to apologize to Alex and that would take some guts. No Lord it will take me relying on you. I realize I was wrong and I need your wisdom to make it right without sounding like I condone their behavior. Please give me the wisdom and balance to love with your love yet stand firm in your precepts. *Okay, I'll man up. It's the godly thing to do anyway.*

Randy walked in the front door and back to the kitchen where Laurie was ironing. He gave her a peck on the cheek. "Time to eat some crow," he said reservedly.

Laurie nodded then said, "Alex is with Tiffy. They're in the TV room." Her gaze narrowed on his face. "Be nice. Remember, he's your future son-in-law."

Randy knew within himself that his apology would carry considerable weight with his daughter and her Alex insofar as his testimony as a father and pastor was concerned. Beside that, he had to make it right for Laurie and Sean's sake as well.

"Hi, dad!" Tiffany said as Randy walked into the TV room.

Alex stood up abruptly from the sofa where they both sat watching a game show and said, "Hello, Mr. Bradshaw."

"Alex, good to see you again," Randy replied. He walked to Tiffany and gave her a kiss then said, "How's my little girl doing today?"

"Much better. Did some walking up and down our block several times today. Trying to get back in shape," she said.

"Can I get either one of you something?" Randy said, giving Alex a surreptitious wink.

Tiffany looked at Alex. "Want anything?"

Alex took the hint. "I'll help you make some coffee."

"Sounds like a plan," Randy said with a smile.

"Is everything all right, Mr. Bradshaw?" Alex asked as he joined him in the kitchen.

Randy motioned to him. "Can I speak to you privately?" Then he whispered the request for coffee in Laurie's ear.

Alex nodded and fell in step behind him as he walked into another room. "Problem?" Alex asked, slightly flustered.

Randy placed his hand on his shoulder. "I need to apologize to you for the accusation I made back at the hospital. I know now that the intimate relationship you had with our daughter was not your idea. Still, I'm sure you realize her mother and I were hurt over this decision because it dishonors God's ways."

Alex filled up, on the verge of tears. "No problem, Mr. Bradshaw," he said in wonder. "Things have been tough for you lately, Mr. Bradshaw, with Tiffany in the hospital and your church responsibilities and everything, so I understand that your finding out would really upset you and Mrs. Bradshaw," he replied. "And just to let you know," he added in contrition, "Tiffany and I discussed this today and we made a pledge to honor the Lord until we get married."

Randy pulled back and took a hard look at the young man before him. His initial assessment of Alex came under immediate review. Many of his preconceived notions about him evaporated into thin air. Now he recognized that he was a man of godly integrity and possessed Christian principles and values. *Okay, he dropped the ball, but now is of a mind to make things right with God and man.* "I'm delighted to hear that Alex. That makes Tiffany's mother and I very happy, and I should add that the Lord will bless you when you honor him."

"Thanks, Mr. Bradshaw," Alex said and extended his hand.

Randy overlooked the handshake and hugged him. "Serve the Lord and take care of my daughter."

"I will do my best."

* * *

Normally by late morning his chronic sinus headache lifted, but not today. The pressure over his right eye caused his eye to water and begin to slowly close. This, along with the pain that ran down his neck to his right shoulder told Randy one thing: go home and nurse this *thorn in the flesh.*

Where is Tiffy's car? he asked himself as he approached his house. *Sean's at school and Laurie is at the church—but where is Tiffany? She is supposed to be convalescing.* He walked into the kitchen and saw a note on the table: 'Feeling better. Need some exercise. Went to the mall and then for lunch.' —Tiffy

"Oooo-ky, great!" he said aloud. *Guess she's feeling better. Excellent!* He turned to use the bathroom and walked past Sean's room. Something told him to stop. Whether or not it was God's Spirit or just plain curiosity he wasn't sure at this point, but he gave the room a visual audit and thought that the tidiness of the room was a bit unusual. The bed was made, his dresser was dusted, and there were no soiled clothes on the floor. He walked over and peeked in his closet and saw that Sean's clothes and shoes were all in order. Several shoeboxes were labeled and the clothes were sectioned off. He was alarmed. *This is very unusual.* Then he thought, *I guess the counseling is working. Praise God! He's getting his life together!* He nodded, deliberately convincing himself.

He turned to exit and at the door he stopped short. He returned to the closet and saw that there were two stacks of shoeboxes, one box on top of the other, but the bottom box in one stack was not labeled. He pulled the box out and opened the lid. "Oh, God!" he exclaimed. What his eyes saw his mind could not believe. There were at least ten unused hypodermic needles, a long strip of rubber band, and six small envelopes with a white powder in them, along with a tablespoon, and a gas cigarette lighter.

His mouth dropped open and his heart began to race. His headache spiraled up and the pain was crushing. He slowly closed the shoebox and returned it to its original hiding place. Suddenly a paralysis swept over him as if a rattlesnake bit him. He froze in place momentarily then slowly walked out of the room, closing the door behind him. He didn't have the presence of mind to think clearly. He groaned in his spirit then several minutes later as the full force of this discovery invaded his whole being leaving him weak and afraid. *I don't know what to do! I don't even know what these drugs are! I'll call Stephanie.*

* * *

"Where is Laurie? Are you alone? I need you to come to my home ASAP!" Randy gulped into his cell phone.

"Laurie is working in the kitchen, preparing the snacks for tonight's youth, and I'm in my office," Stephanie said. "What's the matter? Are you all right, pastor?" her voice rattled, sensing his alarm.

"We've got a huge problem. I found some drugs in Sean's closet and I need you to come and identify them. Obviously he is still using, but this looks very grave," he said anxiously.

"I'll excuse myself and be right over," she said.

"Be discreet," he added and hung up.

* * *

"This looks like heroin," Stephanie said after examining the white powder in the shoebox. She pointed to the other pieces in the box and added ruefully, "And this paraphernalia is common among heroin users."

Randy glanced at her then at the box, but he remained completely still, a statue. Only his eyes moved. "Lord, what is happening?" he lamented. He shook his head then cast his eyes out the window. "How did we get here?"

Stephanie methodically returned the box to its original place and then put her hand on his shoulder and said gently, "He needs healing, pastor. He needs healing."

Randy pounded his fist into his hand and cried out, "He needs divine intervention, that's what he needs!" He rubbed the side of his head momentarily to attenuate some of the sinus pressure that would not yield to his home remedies. Then: "I'm going to call his counselor and let him know what's going on!"

"You sure?" Stephanie said. Dropping her voice— "Interfering?"

He turned on her. "Should I wait until I get a call from the police that my son overdosed? The ME's office?" He pulled out his cell phone. "NO! I'm not waiting."

Stephanie followed him as he walked out of Sean's room into the living room. He dropped into the sofa and as the call progressed he massaged the side of his head. He was miserable.

"Dr. Prentiss' office," the woman answered after seven seconds of digital connections.

Randy unwittingly stood up from the sofa. "This is Pastor Randy from Plantation Gate Church," he said with controlled alarm. Dr. Prentiss is counseling my son, Sean. I need to speak to him right away. It's an emergency."

"I'm sorry Pastor Randy, but he's with a client right now," the receptionist advised.

Randy stiffened. "Would you please slip him a note or something and just have him talk to me for five minutes."

"Hold on. Let me see if I can interrupt him."

"Oh, thank you," Randy said wearily.

What seemed like a never-ending period was only six minutes. "This is Dr. Prentiss, Pastor Randy. How can I help you?" Randy heard.

"Dr. Prentiss—" he broke off to catch his breath. "—I just discovered that my son, Sean is doing hard drugs! I believe he's on heroin. What should I do?"

After many years of experience in counseling those with all forms of addiction, Dr. Prentiss could tell if the threat was real. "Pastor Randy, you know that I'm limited in what I am legally able to share with you out of confidentiality, but because you're a pastor and his father, I can tell you that your son has confided in me that he has used drugs in the past, but he also told me that he has kept clean since he's been seeing me."

Randy breathed a sigh of relief. "Do you believe him?"

"I am compelled to take him at his verbal testimony," Dr. Prentiss replied.

"But I found what looks like heroin and stuff in his bedroom closet," Randy argued.

"That doesn't mean he's using now, does it?"

"No, I guess not," Randy reasoned. "But then again, if he's clean, why would he even have it nearby unless he planed to use it in the future?"

Dr. Prentiss realized Randy frustration and helplessness. "We don't know for sure. We can only trust that our counseling sessions will bring about a change in his view toward illegal drugs and in turn change his lifestyle."

"I'm getting very worried, Dr. Prentiss," Randy said dolefully. "Should I say anything to him?"

"My advice, Pastor Randy, is to let God's Spirit work in Sean's life to bring about the resolution in this crisis. I can hear the anxiety in your voice, but these forms of addiction are extremely tenacious and you must wait until he is ready to give the drugs up. If you attempt to interfere or intervene, he may not only stop coming for counseling, but will do the drugs on the sneak. This has to be a 'God-thing.'"

Dr. Prentiss' words hit Randy in the heart. He was right. He had to back off and let God work this out. "So I should just ignore this whole thing?"

"Let me handle this from my end. He's coming for his next session in two days. At that time I'll dig deeper and approach the subject from a different perspective and after that I will discuss with him the possibility of giving you some sort of assurance that he's really trying and has a measure of success." He paused then, "I have to get back to my session, but as for you, Pastor Randy, try not to worry. God will work this all out."

"Bless you, Dr. Prentiss," Randy said appreciatively and clicked off. A wave of calm crept slowly over him.

"What did he say?" Stephanie asked impatiently.

Randy rubbed the back of his neck. His headache remained despite the good counsel. "He said that I shouldn't worry and that he's aware that Sean has a drug problem, but said that Sean told him he was *clean*. He will continue to explore the cause and effect and assured me that God will work things out."

Stephanie smiled. "Praise the Lord for good Christian counseling." She made her way to the front door then paused and asked, "Have you brought Laurie into this problem yet?"

He bit his lower lip. "Not yet."

Stephanie shook her head and walked out.

Randy stroked his sinus passages but his headache would not lift.

* * *

Panic-stricken, he hurried through the ER entrance of Plantation General and stopped short as he looked at the duty nurse behind the counter. "Where is my son, Sean Bradshaw?" he exclaimed nervously.

The nurse pointed toward a corridor. Flustered: "He's in bay five."

"Lord, let him not die!" he cried out as he raced down the hallway. Seconds later he walked into the ER cubicle. He gaped in disbelief as he saw two doctors and one nurse hovering over Sean as he lay in the bed. One doctor was injecting a fluid into his IV while the other doctor held a stethoscope to Sean's heart. He was shaking his head. The ER nurse held her hand to her mouth and began to cry. "He's the same age as my son," he heard her say as she started to sob.

"Sean!" Randy yelled. "Hold on!"

"SEAN! I'm coming!" Laurie hollered as she rushed to his side with Tiffany and Stephanie behind her.

The doctors exchanged glances and moved to one side of his bed while the nurse detached the monitors. "I'm sorry, Mr. and Mrs. Bradshaw, but we were too late," one of the doctors said sorrowfully. "When he came in we immediately began to flush his system of the drugs—but if only we had more time—"

"Oh, no, dear God, NO!" Laurie shrieked.

Stephanie reached over and clutched Tiffany to hold her up as her knees began to buckle under her. "I'm so sorry for you," she said through tears.

When she looked over at Randy he was facing the cubicle wall and started pounding it. "My God, why have you forsaken me?" he cried surging with grief.

The doctors nodded to the nurse and slowly retreated from the cubicle. The nurse paused at the entrance and closed the curtain behind her. Laurie stood at Sean's bedside then grabbed his and kissed it. "Why did you leave us?" she sobbed.

Randy whirled and stepped over to her, engulfing her in his arms. He said nothing. He just held her until they both stopped crying.

* * *

The sanctuary was filled with congregants and family alike. Many school friends and neighbors came as well. On the altar and on the floor next to the pulpit were floral pieces, sprays, and photographs of Sean with his family and friends. Randy and Laurie sat in the pew next to their son's casket, while in the lobby Tiffany and Stephanie continued to welcome the latecomers as they waited for the signal that the service was about to begin.

Randy looked over at Sean's pallbearers. He saw Alex along with his brother and the other two were college buddies that wanted to be part of Sean's goodbye. In the pew to his right sat his staff and deacons, each one of them carrying the message on their faces of their deep sorrow.

Randy nodded to the funeral director who in turn waved him on to give his son's eulogy with a gospel message.

Lord, only you can get me through this.

* * *

At the gravesite, all the close family and friends slowly marched to Sean's casket and placed a rose on it. They lingered for a time and cried. After one hour, only the Bradshaw's and Stephanie remained.

* * *

He sat in the car of the Sunset Garden Cemetery and slowly opened the envelope, carefully removing one of the death certificates. His eyes focused on the line that said *NAME OF DECEASED*. It was his son's name: *Sean Bradshaw*. He began to weep. Tears streamed down his face as he read his age, address, and occupation at time of death. Then came the hard part: *CAUSE:* Acute combined drug intoxication.

He wiped the tears from his eyes and returned the death certificate to the envelope and then let his head fall back on the headrest.

He just closed his eyes and cried uncontrollably.

* * *

He felt himself. He was awake and in a cold sweat and when he lifted his head off his pillow, it was wet from tears. His headache was lifting but he found it hard to breathe. He was emotionally exhausted and full of anxiety. "It was a dream!" he said aloud. "It was all a dream!" He climbed out of his bed and lumbered to the bathroom and then took a hot shower to help alleviate the headache and after fifteen minutes, he was free of it.

* * *

TWELVE

It seemed like an interminable period of time, but in reality, only ten seconds had passed before Dr. Prentiss picked up his phone. "Hello, Pastor Randy," he said. "My secretary said your call sounded urgent."

With his wireless desk phone in hand, Randy walked to his office door and slowly closed it. "Sorry to bother you so early in the morning Dr. Prentiss, but I needed to talk to you about something."

"Okay. Is this about your son?"

"In a way, yes, but not totally," he replied in anticipation. "You see, I had this terrible dream— actually a nightmare— about him yesterday afternoon and I didn't want to tell anybody about it except you."

"Sounds ominous," Dr. Prentiss replied. "Tell me about it."

Randy's breath caught in his throat. "Well, in short, Sean died of a drug overdose. It really upset me. There was a lot of detail—"

"Well you know how dreams are, Pastor Randy," Dr. Prentiss soothed, "they can be very frightening and alarming, yet, in reality, most of them never come to pass."

"Well, for some godforsaken reason, I thought that maybe it was a premonition of some kind."

"Now, now, let's not get freaky on me," Dr. Prentiss said. "I wouldn't be too concerned about it. Just try to rest in the Lord and take your mind off your son for a while."

"I would need a lobotomy in order to take my mind off him," Randy noted dryly.

"Maybe you should share this dream—or nightmare if you will, with your wife. Maybe that would help alleviate some of the stress you're going through," Dr. Prentiss suggested.

"Hmm, yes. Um," he stalled. "I suppose I could."

"Well, first let me ask if you have discussed *anything* about Sean's drug history with her? It sounds like your hesitant," Dr. Prentiss queried.

"Not yet. I'm waiting for the right time."

"I see. Well, I wouldn't wait too long," he urged. "These things have a way of coming around and biting us in the backside."

"No, no," Randy insisted, "it's on my 'to-do' list for this week."

Dr. Prentiss acquired the gift of discernment early in his Christian life and counted it an important gift when counseling. "Let me ask you this, Pastor Randy," he started. "You're not blaming yourself for this situation that Sean is in, are you?"

"Not sure what you mean," Randy replied.

"When parents discover that their son or daughter has turned the wrong way and exhibit sinful behavior, they often blame themselves," he explained. "I'm sure you've heard the old expression 'where did we go wrong?' when a parent finds out their kids are in trouble because they believe they raised them correctly."

"It has certainly crossed my mind," Randy said.

"Just to put your mind and conscience at rest," Dr. Prentiss expounded, "Sean's sin nature drew him away from God's will and into this dark world he's now in. He made his own decision to engage in addictive drugs and must come to the place where he recognizes the commensurate consequences that go along with those decisions." He stopped then summarized: "His sin is not your sin."

"I'm at the point in my life where I am so vulnerable—I find myself questioning myself constantly about everything," Randy admitted. "So when this nightmare occurred, I just lost it."

"Perhaps this dream is a cue from the Lord for you to go talk to Sean."

"But I thought you wanted me to wait—"

"At first I did, but in view of this development, I think you should go talk to him," Dr. Prentiss advised. "What's the worst that could happen? He gets mad at you? No, if I were you I would talk to him and tell him about your dream."

"I'll take this as godly counsel. Thank you, Dr. Prentiss," Randy said and ended the call.

* * *

The ride to the house was anything but relaxing. As a pastor, family confrontation always set his teeth on edge despite his pastoral counseling skills that seem to work with others better than with his own family. *A prophet is without honor in his own home, right?* he thought. *Timing is important*, he reasoned further. *I want to talk to him when he first gets home from school, when there's no one else in the house.*

He rehearsed his opening lines, then he ticked off in his mind the salient points he had to make. *Remember,* he reminded himself, *don't preach to him. Just talk to him: father to son.* That was his plan.

He sat at the kitchen table with a cup of coffee and nibbled on biscotti while periodically looking out the window. *Where are you, Sean?* Twenty-five minutes advanced to forty-five minutes. No Sean. He stood up and paced about the kitchen then pulled out his cell phone. With his finger poised over Sean's speed dial number he paused. *No, I'm not going to give him advance warning.* He replaced his phone on his belt. "Something is wrong," he whispered to himself. "He's never this late." He checked his wristwatch again. Sean was now one hour overdue.

All at once Sean's vehicle pulled rapidly into the driveway.

"Whoa! Driving a little fast, Sean," Randy said aloud. Sean jumped out of his vehicle and rushed toward the front door in a zigzag pattern.

The door flung open!

"Uh. What's going on, dad?" he said as he slowly closed the door.

"I came home early to talk to you," Randy replied, waving him toward the kitchen table. "We need to talk."

Sean's face contorted in silent protest. "Ooookay" he said and slowly sat down opposite his father.

Randy placed his two hands on the table and began to rub them together as he gathered his thoughts. "I'm not quite sure how to say this, Sean, but I've been very troubled over you and need to talk to you." He stopped rubbing his hands and looked deeply into Sean's eyes.

"What about?"

"Well, I had this dream about you last night and it really upset me," he said, attempting to control his emotions. He paused, then: "It was more like a nightmare."

Sean fidgeted in his chair then began nibbling on his fingernails. "Sounds scary," he said glibly.

"Sean, this is serious!" Randy said bristling, latching on to one of Sean's hands.   Then he blurted out: "In my dream you died of an overdose!"

"Look, dad," he said curtly. "If I were doing drugs, I wouldn't be able to function." He stopped and mechanically buttoned his long sleeve shirt. "If I were doing drugs, I wouldn't be able to do my school work, right?" He pointed out the window and raised his voice one octave. "I wouldn't be able to drive, even!"

"There are functioning addicts, Sean," Randy argued. A tear formed in his right eye. "Sean, we love you and care for you. I just don't want you to do anything foolish that would put your life in jeopardy."

"Dad," he sighed with resignation, "I'm okay."

Randy's limited counseling experience dictated that addicts will squirm out of truth and deny their dependence on illegal substances in order to divert from admitting use, but with his own son, he could not take any chances. "What evidence can you give me that you're clean?"

Sean threw his arms up in the air. "I'm going to counseling, right? What more do you want from me?" He stood up and pushed his chair back. "How much proof do you need? *I told you I'm not using.* If you don't believe me, that's your problem!" With that he walked defiantly down the hall into his bedroom and slammed the door.

Randy unconsciously lowered his head into his hands as suspicion crept into his heart. "Lord, is he lying to me? Help us!"

* * *

He raised his head when he heard the garage door open automatically. He turned and looked out the kitchen window to see Laurie pulling in the driveway with Tiffany following behind her. He took a deep breath and shot a prayer up to heaven that God would intervene. In his gut he just thought that things were going to spiral downward very quickly unless God stepped in. What he didn't know was that the Lord, indeed, was orchestrating the events to expose the family secret.

"Home early, dad?" Tiffany asked as she rounded the corner into the kitchen.

Randy nodded as Laurie walked in after her. "Hi," he said to them, swallowing hard.

Laurie read her husband's face. "What's the matter?"

He shook his head and waved her off. "Nothing."

She walked over next to him and sat down. "Doesn't look like 'nothing,'" she said.

Tiffany scoped the kitchen and the adjoining dining room as she sat down at the table. "Where's Sean?"

Randy turned and pointed. "He's in his room."

Laurie sensed trouble. "What's going on?"

"I'LL TELL YOU WHAT THE HELL IS GOING ON!" Sean yelled from behind. He stood in the doorway pointing to his father. "He thinks I'm—he used a profanity—doing drugs!"

Tiffany covered her mouth in horror. "SEAN!" she cried out. "Watch your mouth!"

Laurie shook her head and jumped up from the table then focused on Randy. "What's all this?"

Sean staggered into the middle of the kitchen. "'What's all this'?" he snarled as he pointed to his mother. "It's so like *Laurie* to *not* know what's going on!"

"THAT'S ENOUGH, SEAN!" Randy bellowed.

"Oh—really, Randy?" he mocked. Then he performed a dance step then: "…you boff meke me seck. It's 'bout time you boff tok your heds from your butts and pade atten-tion to wats going on in your own home!" He dropped to the floor in a heap. "All da time at da church." He looked up and turned to his mother. "…You shud be stay-ing home!"

Laurie held her hand to her forehead as tears stung her eyes. "Randy, is he drunk?"

"He's high on drugs! That's what's going on!" Tiffany exclaimed.

"THAT'S ENOUGH, SEAN!" Randy repeated as he stood up from the table and grabbed his arm to pull him up.

"ET cud liv here, *Laurie*, and you woo-dn't even know it" Sean said in a moment of lucidity as he stood up, shaking. Then he slapped his knee and burst out into laughter. "Ha! Ha! —some fam-i-ly we are!" he said with a devilish guffaw then rushed to the countertop and yanked on the toaster. It crashed to the floor.

Laurie covered her ears and backed up against the kitchen wall. "Randy, do something!" she gasped.

Randy jumped behind him and held his hands and turned to Tiffany. "I'VE HAD ENOUGH!" he shouted and tightened his grip. "Tiffy, call the police!"

"NO!" Laurie screamed. "Randy, no! Keep it here!"

Tiffany went for the phone as Sean forcefully squirmed away from his father's grasp. "That's real cooo-l," he said and swore vehemently.

Tiffany stomped her foot on the floor. "SEAN!" she screamed then threw the phone at him. "GET OUT OF THIS HOUSE!"

The phone hit him in the head, dazing him momentarily. "Now that's rrr-eal Christ-yan luv!" he snarled back mockingly.

Laurie, her heart breaking, ran to her son and cried, "Sean, what's happening to you? I'm your mom; I love you and want to help you! Please Sean, talk to me, and help me understand what you're going through so I can try to help." With tears running down her face Laurie contemplated her son. A thousand thoughts went through her mind. *Were there signs? Why didn't I see them? Did I fail him? What should I do?* "Sean, let dad and I get you into a rehab center. We will go though this with you. You are not alone—the Lord promises never to leave you or forsake you."

"LEAVE ME ALONE!" Sean shouted and dashed to his room, locking the door behind him.

Laurie collapsed into a chair while Randy paced the floor. Tiffany just stood staring down the hallway to Sean's bedroom.

Moments later Sean stumbled out of his bedroom with his backpack in hand and raced to the front door. He glanced into the kitchen and bared his teeth in a smile. "Good-bye, family!"

"Sean, don't go!" Randy and Laurie begged. "We want to help you!"

He looked at them with disdain then slammed the door after him.

Seconds afterward they heard his car pull out and careen down the street.

Randy walked to Laurie as she stood up and hugged her while motioning for Tiffany to join them. They stood motionless until Randy pulled away and rushed to Sean's room heading straight for his closet. When he looked into the unlabeled shoebox, it was empty.

* * *

"When were you going to tell me about all of this?" Laurie demanded as Randy walked back into the kitchen.

"I thought I could spare you this mess," he said dolefully. "Obviously it was not meant to be. I was hoping that Sean would be well into recovery and then when you were told it would be history. It would all be behind us." He started to groan from within then added, "He's been in counseling, but apparently that's not working—" he stopped short. "I'm afraid..."he trailed off.

"Afraid of what?" Laurie asked pointedly.

"I had this dream that he overdosed," he said and started to whimper. "I called his counselor about it and he told me that nightmares don't amount to much and that I should talk to Sean about it. He assured me that he was not using drugs at the time." He shook his head in disgust. "My confronting him is what started all of this."

Laurie walked slowly to the counter and put on a pot of coffee, then walked to the hallway and called out, "Tiffany, I need you here to help us sort this out." Moments later Tiffany walked into the kitchen from her bedroom with a handkerchief to her nose and tears streaming down her face.

"How long have you two known about Sean's addiction?" Laurie said roughly.

"We discovered the problem about three weeks ago," Randy said in their defense.

She poured herself a cup of coffee and gestured to Randy and Tiffany to get their own. "Tell me everything," she said and sat down at the table.

For the next hour Randy and Tiffany recounted to Laurie the events of Sean's journey into the dark world of illegal drug addiction. Then Laurie sighed with resignation, collected her handbag and car keys and then silently walked out the front door.

Immobilized for several moments, Randy then lifted his cell phone from his belt and called Dr. Prentiss. Tiffany cried all the way back to her bedroom.

* * *

Laurie sat on a Plantation Park bench under an arbor and gazed off into the distance at the setting sun as it momentarily hovered over the horizon, casting resplendent rays of golden light over the Everglades. It was her favorite time of the day. For her it was a special time for reflection on what she had accomplished for the day and to plan for tomorrow. But today was different. *Today I am in pain. Severe pain. Lord, what am I to do? I can't think about tomorrow, I can only think on this moment. I'm afraid of tomorrow.* "My family is falling apart and I feel helpless," she whispered to herself. "Father God, I am angry at Randy and Tiffany. That's just an excuse that they wanted to protect me. Now that the problem is full blown they dump it on me.

"Why did Sean lash out at me, Lord? I have always been there for him, perhaps too interested in the every day going on in his life. Help me Father to settle my thoughts and remove the anger from my heart so we can face this crisis together as a family and glorify you."

She turned her head and focused on the *Passiflora incarnate* vine growing aggressively on the arbor and took notice of two butterflies laying eggs on the underside of the leaves. She stared at them for several minutes then was drawn to other butterfly eggs that had progressed from eggs to caterpillars to the chrysalis stage—the final stage before the butterfly is reborn and it flies away only to renew the cycle. "Lord, my heart is broken," she whispered somberly. "I need you to *cocoon* me from this horror in my family." Tears began to run down her face. "Yes Lord, that's what I am asking, that you *cocoon* me from what lies ahead so that I can face whatever trouble you have ordained for our family, and that I will be strong and not cave in. That I will be able to support my Randy and Tiffany through this storm."

When I am afraid, I will trust in you, she sang to God in her heart. She turned away and fixated on the lingering aura of the setting sun and welled up inside and prayed wearily, "Lord, I ask for mercy on my family. I ask that you give my Randy the wisdom and guidance he needs to direct our family and please grant him the understanding to deal with our Sean."

Darkness set in. Laurie returned to her car then drove aimlessly around her neighborhood until the realization came over her that Randy and Tiffany needed her at home.

* * *

Almost mechanical-like, Laurie walked into the house to see Randy standing in the middle of the kitchen with a pot in his hand. She smiled mirthlessly but his face lit up when their eyes met. "Been praying for you since you left," he said.

"Needed to spend some time alone with God," she replied.

Randy nodded. "Understand, perfectly. Doing better?"

"Working at it," she said and strode back to the kitchen table and sat down. "Tiffy?"

Randy gestured. "In her room."

"Dinner?"

"Have three chicken breasts and potatoes in the oven," he said holding up the pot and added, "mixed vegetables?"

Laurie nodded again.

"Made a call to Sean's counselor after you left," Randy began. "When I told Dr. Prentiss what happened he said that Sean missed his counseling session this week and that he was concerned. Then he said he would try to contact him and call me afterward."

Laurie's eyebrows shot up. "Maybe we'll get some encouraging news?"

"May it be so."

Tiffany walked out of her bedroom cuddling one of her Teddy bears and then walked to her mother and hugged her with the bear dangling in her hand. "I love you, mom," she said softly.

"I love you, too," Laurie said, squeezing her slightly.

Randy stood still as they embraced, his eyes watering as his emotions flared up once again. "We must believe God," he stated in a prayer-like fashion, "that this crisis has a greater purpose, and that it will bring glory to his Name. In the meantime, we must trust the Lord."

They all agreed to trust the Lord then sat at the table for dinner, but their appetites were very muted.

* * *

Randy was resting in his recliner when the call from Dr. Prentiss finally came. He sat erect and then put his cell phone on speaker. "Pastor Randy," Dr. Prentiss said, "I finally contacted Sean on his cell phone," he began.

Laurie and Tiffany were sitting on the sofa struggling with their emotions. Laurie inclined her ear as Tiffany squeezed her Teddy bear. It had been a long two hours since Randy telephoned him about Sean.

"We're here, Dr. Prentiss. I have you on speaker phone," Randy said.

"My heart goes out to your family at this time of crisis," Dr. Prentiss soothed.

"Thank you," they all said in unison.

"Well, he didn't tell me where he is at the present, and attempting to counsel over the phone is very difficult because you cannot see the person's face or body signals that often helps to evaluate their responses. But I took a hard posture with him and rebuked him for his behavior and told him to take responsibility for his actions."

"How did he sound?" Laurie asked. "Did he sound like he was 'high'?"

"To some extent, yes," Dr. Prentiss said. "My assessment is that he's on his way 'down' from his drug euphoria."

"Did he recommit to counseling?" Randy asked, longingly. He was of the persuasion that if Sean recommitted, there was hope of rehabilitation.

"He said that he would think about returning to counseling. That in and of itself is not conclusive since he is not totally lucid at this time. But take heart, I believe he will come around," Dr. Prentiss added optimistically.

Tiffany's face brightened. "Dr. Prentiss, this is Tiffany, his sister. If he calls you please tell him we love him and miss him."

"I will be sure to do that," he assured her. Seconds later he cleared his throat and explained: "I needed to take the crisis at hand as a divine opportunity to get tough with him after awhile."

"Oh!" Randy blurted. "What happened?"

"We had covered many issues in our sessions, but I had to reiterate to Sean that he cannot blame others for his poor choices."

Startled, Laurie asked, "He's not blaming his parents, is he?"

"Mrs. Bradshaw, you have to understand that in his present state, he blames everybody and everything but himself for his problems."

Laurie began to cry. "We have been very good to our son, Dr. Prentiss. And there is no cause for him to blame us for his problems."

"It's not his family's fault that he made poor choices in his life! His lifestyle and friends are the cause of his problems, not us!" Tiffany glowered and said bluntly.

Randy gestured to Tiffany to back off with her attitude. "Dr. Prentiss, what should we do now?"

"There's not a whole lot you can do now, Pastor Randy. If Sean belongs to God, God will intervene at some point and bring him around," he noted. "Let's agree to turn him over to the Lord and wait for him to contact you. If he contacts me, I will alert you immediately."

Randy sighed. "Then we'll leave it there for now." He turned to Laurie and Tiffany. "We need to pray for our Sean." Tiffany burst out into tears once again.

* * *

THIRTEEN

There were several half-eaten fast food containers strewn all over the kitchen counter, but it didn't seem to matter. A band of cockroaches were feasting on the random food droppings that spotted the kitchen floor, but it didn't seem to matter. The living room shades were drawn and the room was dark, even during the day—with only a twenty-five watt lamp illuminating it—but it didn't seem to matter. The carpet in the room was stained and gave off a reeky odor of cat urine, but it didn't seem to matter. The toilet in the apartment bathroom ran day and night, but it didn't seem to matter, either. The only thing that mattered to George and Sean is that their beds were free of vermin and that their drugs were within arms reach.

"Your turn to call in the pizza order, Sean," George said, squinting at him. He looked over at him lying on the living room sofa, coming out of his high and into some semblance of normalcy.

Sean slowly sat up and ruffled his hair and waited a moment for his vision to clear. "What time is it?"

George peered at the wall clock. "Four-thirty in the afternoon."

Sean kicked the cat off his feet as the feline rubbed herself against him, purring for attention. "How long has it been?"

George shook his head and chuckled softly. "Long time, I guess."

"Losing track of time," Sean conceded.

"No matter," George said, throwing his arms up in the air. "What diff—?" Then he snapped his fingers. "Easy on my cat."

"Yeah, right," Sean replied. He stood up and pulled his wallet out of his pocked to check his cash. "Need some help to pay for the pizza," he said matter-of-factly.

George nodded then walked to his bedroom to get the money as Sean flipped open his cell phone to make the call. When he looked at the phone, there were five missed calls from his father and two text messages from his sister. He read the text messages that pleaded for him to call her, but he deleted them before calling in the pizza order. He completely ignored the calls from his father, deliberately putting him out of his mind.

* * *

Stephanie interpreted Laurie's phone message as a 'distress call' more than anything else. With an urgent desire to help and with keen discernment she immediately returned the call. "Laurie, I got your message. What's going on?"

"Sean's in trouble, Stephanie. Can we meet to talk?"

"Say where and when," Stephanie replied with rising concern.

"I'd rather not meet at our church, so let's meet in the pavilion at Markham Park in fifteen minutes."

"Done!" Stephanie said and ended the call. *Pastor Randy's family needs help. I just know it in my heart.*

* * *

Laurie drove slowly through the serpentine road at Markham Park past the picnic and camping sights and the ball fields until it dead-ended at the park pavilion. As she pulled into the parking lot she noticed that Stephanie was sitting in her car, waiting.

Laurie waved her out and walked over to a bench under a Purple Jacaranda tree. She pulled out a tissue from her bag and wiped down the bench as Stephanie walked up. "You all right?" Stephanie asked. Laurie turned to face her. When Stephanie saw her swollen eyes and steaming tears she cried out, "Oh, my God! What's the matter?"

Laurie breathed heavily as she sobbed, "It's Sean. He's on drugs . . . and he—" she began to retch—"left the house and we don't know where he is or . . ." her voice faded as her shoulders rose and fell uncontrollably with her sobbing and retching.

"Easy now, Laurie," Stephanie whispered as she sat next to her and stroked her arm. "Easy now." She held her close and shot a prayer for help up to the Lord.

A full five minutes of anxiety and emotional tension finally passed. Then as she began to settle: "Randy told me he knew from the beginning about Sean's addiction, but I just found out and I'm having—"

"—a tough time of it," Stephanie finished her sentence. "Yes, from my experience in the homeless ministry I know all about drug addiction and what devastation it brings."

Laurie's tears slowed to a trickle. "I know you do. That's why I needed to come to you alone so you could help me with this." The memories of Stephanie's testimonies about her interaction and counsel to the homeless who lost everything due to illegal drug abuse were now ever-present in Laurie's mind.

"I need to tell you something," Stephanie said, pulling back to look straight at her. She scanned her face. "I knew about Sean's problem with drugs for quite some time. Randy came to me when he first learned about it."

"You did?" she said incredulously. "Who else knew about it?"

Stephanie bit her lower lip. "Beside Randy and I, only Tiffany." She shook her head. "Randy wanted to keep it contained—to keep it from you and the church—hoping the problem would go away in a short while. He really wanted to spare you the pain a mother feels with these things." *The Lord does not limit joy, but does limit pain,* she thought.

"Well, it's not contained and the whole thing has backfired in the Bradshaw's family face," she added with a wounded look.

Stephanie sat erect then said didactically, "You must steel yourself during this trial or it will destroy you and your family. It may be a while before it's over. You have to be strong."

"I've asked the Lord to cocoon me, but it's easier said than done."

Stephanie nodded in support and then added, "Drug addiction is serious business, even in the church, because there are several enemies to battle. Satan is the number one bad guy who has his hand in anything that has to do with drugs, and I might add sex. Then there's our modern drug culture that classifies many addictive drugs as *recreational,* making it sound like fun to smoke crack and pot and to take pills to go up and then back down. Then there's the 'date-rape' drugs, along with the 'pill mill' doctors who prescribe pain medication to anyone who asks for it.

"Unfortunately, the drug problem is escalating, and in fact, Revelation 9:21 hints that drug abuse continues throughout the Seal judgments which is more than half way through the Tribulation period. So this plague on America is not going away."

Laurie hid her face in her hands. "Why has this come upon us? Why is God allowing this?" she moaned as tears began to flow once again. "We have been faithful in serving God, so why is he punishing us? First it was Tiffany's tumor, now it's Sean's drug problem. Why, Lord? Why?"

Stephanie remembered reading that Luther said at one time, *A true believer will crucify the question, 'Why?' They will obey without question.* But this was hardly the time to mention that creed since it seemed almost impossible to live life without asking God for answers when in pain. Even Christ asked His Father from the Cross-, 'Why have you forsaken me?' And David, the man after God's own heart asked during severe trials,

'Why Lord?' "It's better that we don't ask 'why' Laurie," Stephanie entreated. "Something's are better left unasked when it comes to God's ways."

Laurie sniffled. "How did you survive when you were leaving your old life of homelessness and starting a new life with Christ—I mean how did you make it when it came to trusting God?"

Stephanie's eyes suddenly brightened. Her eyes probed deeply into Laurie's. "I forced myself to remember every morning the three 'I wills.' Number one, *I will* not doubt. Number two, *I will* trust the Lord, and number three, *I will* believe the Lord. That has been my mantra since the time of my salvation."

Laurie kneaded her temples then expelled a sigh. "It certainly seems to be working."

"Over the years I have added to that refrain, that I—" she stopped short then added while slicing her hand horizontally and incrementally in the air, "—will never, *never*, NEVER, doubt the Lord again."

"May it be so with me," Laurie prayed.

Stephanie patted Laurie's hand several times. "You'll see, God will work this all out for his glory."

Laurie's cell phone chimed with a text message.

She pulled the cell phone from her handbag and glanced at it. "Oh, my God!" she exclaimed, "it's from Sean."

"Good news, I hope," Stephanie noted dryly.

Laurie read the message then squeezed her eyes shut and said haltingly, "This is a message from hell!"

"What does is say?" Stephanie said, watching with piercing eyes.

"He's calling Randy and I all kinds of names and blaming us for his horrible life," Laurie said in shock and disbelief.

"I've seen this behavior before," Stephanie observed.

"And after all we've done for him," Laurie lamented. "That he would turn on his own parents—" her voice broke up. "—Unbelievable."

"Unbelievable, I know," Stephanie echoed.

* * *

Randy sat in his office gazing out the window, totally immersed in the family secret that he believed if exposed could bring down his ministry. Pastors with a son who is a drug addict were not too popular when it came to church politics and certainly lost credibility when it came to preaching about family integrity and separation to holiness. He stood up and starting pacing the floor while staring down at the carpet then walked back to his desk, sat down in his chair, his shoulders hunched, and wept. "Lord, help," he cried softly.

"Pastor Randy," he heard. "Pastor Mike is here to see you," Susan said from outside his office door.

"Be right there," he replied after clearing his throat. He pulled a handkerchief from his rear pocket and dabbed his eyes before walking to the small mirror hanging on the wall next to the door. "Clean yourself up, Bradshaw," he whispered to himself. Seconds later he opened the door.

"Good morning, pastor," Mike said as he walked in. "Doing okay?" he asked before looking at him.

"I've been better," Randy said as he closed the door. "In truth, I'm *not* having a good day."

Mike looked intently at him, zeroing in on his eyes. "I can see what you mean. Family situation worsened?"

Randy nodded and pointed to a chair. "Yes, brother, things have worsened. The notion of keeping our family secret about Sean's drug problem has blown up in my face. Some might call it a setback but the way this unfolded, I call it a major reversal."

"What happened?"

"I went to talk to him as his dad, and told him about this nightmare I had where he died of an overdose and he *freaked out*! Then Laurie and Tiffany came home and he came out of his bedroom 'high' and then an argument erupted. Then when we questioned him he flew into a rage then stormed out of the house to parts unknown." He slowly and silently circled his desk, then: "I'm at the end, Mike. I just don't know what to do. My family is falling apart and I feel helpless to do anything about it."

Mike went deeply pensive for several moments. "Pastor you know this church loves you and your family. They have demonstrated their love over the years by supporting your ideas and giving your free reign to run this church. Now its time you treated them like the family of God. They have laughed with you and now is a time of mourning and prayer. Don't you think they will be before the throne for Sean's sake?" He paused and added, "Your family is under attack from the other side. We should have the congregation pray for you and your family and ask for deliverance from the Evil One's hold on Sean."

Randy nodded, hearing what he said, not agreeing with his advice. "I'm afraid of that," he admitted. "Just afraid that—"

Redeemed how I love to proclaim it . . . His cell phone rang out.

"It's Laurie," he said. "I have to take this."

Mike waved his approval. "Of course."

Randy walked toward a corner of his office as Mike closed his eyes, seemingly praying. The next five minutes were tense as Mike watched Randy's face contort as he conversed with Laurie. Then he shut his phone and said, "Laurie received a 'hate' text message from Sean blaming us for his horrible life." He shook his head in disgust and then sat down at his desk.

Mike read his face. "Ugh." he said then closed his eyes momentarily and asked God for divine guidance. *What do I say to my pastor who is under attack from evil forces at a time when he is undergoing a family crisis? How can I minister to him? I cannot tell him the real reason I came to see him: the congregation is mystified over his behavior and many are asking questions about his family. What do I say? Should I say to those asking questions that it's because he is consumed with Sean when this is not my story to tell?* He thought otherwise and walked to Randy and put his hand on his shoulder and said, "Pastor, this problem is too great for you and your family. We need more prayer warriors to storm the Throne Room and beg the Lord for Sean's deliverance! If you don't want to ask the whole congregation, perhaps we should just bring in a small representative slice of the faithful to join the staff in prayer and fasting before God."

Randy blinked. His spirit testified that Mike's suggestion was a worthy one. A surge of hope swept over him. "Mike, that's a great plan! We can choose a contained group to pray for my family while not involving the rest of the church." He stood up and added, "I want to run it by Laurie and hear what she thinks about it."

Mike nodded. "Good. Let me know what Laurie says and then we can both select who we would include." He returned to his chair and with the confidence of accomplishing a reprieve from a sorrowful visit, said, "On other matters, pastor, Van Fleming seems to be stirring up the pot. He's obviously made some phone calls to a few folks and has taken some kind of poll regarding your sermons and it seems he's attracted a few 'disgruntled' members who agree with him that you should soften your homilies."

"Rats," he said and then grumped, "I need to get him in here and have a heart-to-heart talk with him before he goes too far."

"Let me know if I can help, pastor," Mike said as he exited Randy's office.

Randy felt an upwelling of relief. The thought of group prayer for his family without embroiling the rest of the church was a welcome one. He looked up. "Thank you, Lord," he said in praise then walked out of his office to Susan's desk. "Call Mr. Van Fleming and ask him to make an appointment for us to talk."

Susan's eyebrows shot up. "Problems?"

"Just a slight tremor. Not an earthquake." Then he turned and asked, "Has Laurie and Stephanie come in yet?"

Susan nodded. "They just came in. They're making coffee in the kitchen."

"That's what I need now," he said with a chuckle, "a strong cup of coffee and something made with lots of sugar."

* * *

It was early evening and the sun was low in the horizon as he slowly opened the front door and carefully lifted the cats placing them outside and closed the door. Then he walked into the bedroom and glanced over at George lying asleep in his bed. "Sleep on, friend," he said. "See you on the other side." From there he stepped into the living room and opened up his backpack and set up his stuff on the small table in front of the sofa.

Moments after the injection he heard a ringing in his ears. *I hate that sound!* A slight pause, then: *was that the doorbell?* He started to stand up to answer the door, but fell back on the sofa. *You're hearing things, Sean.* He stretched out on the sofa and turned his ear to the front door. *Cats meowing? Cats howling?* He slapped the side of his head then shook it for several seconds until a smile emerged on his face. "Beautiful," he said, then reached over and lifted George's pack of cigarettes off the table and lit one up. He stretched his feet out and rested them on the table. "Now this is living!" he exclaimed before extinguishing the cigarette.

Ten minutes passed then he stood up but began to wobble in place. He dropped back into the sofa then slapped the side of his head again then stood up once more and walked to the kitchen. He poured himself two shot glasses of bourbon from the bottle on the counter and smiled. "No pain, and no gain," he chortled and slugged them down.

He staggered momentarily then zigzagged back to the sofa and plopped down. It seemed a long time to traverse the distance. "Ah, this feels good," he said aloud. He heard scratching at the door. "Go away!" he yelled out. *Getting tense, Sean,* he told himself. *Starting to come down already. Maybe—?* He gazed down at his stuff and his heart began to race. *Go for it!*

* * *

Am I dreaming?

Suddenly surreal images shot into his mind! He saw himself in utter darkness falling down a bottomless shaft. He clutched the bottom of the chair in which he was sitting to gain some semblance of reality but it brought no relief. Hurtling downward he tried to grasp the sides of the shaft to slow his descent but they remained out of reach. "Help!" he bellowed out. "I'm falling!"

After an interminable period of time, his downward motion slowed until he stood on a precipice overlooking a vast cavernous abyss. "Where am I?" he gasped in horror. He turned his head to listen as a strident buzzing sound came up from below, then millions of insect-like creatures ascended from the pit and whizzed past him. He stepped back as the swarms seemed to envelop him before continuing their journey. "HELP ME!" he shrieked.

"You are in the place where no one returns," a voice from behind said in a yowling cry.

He turned toward the sound to see a grotesque creature with six wings, two extended above his head, with the other four folded on his back. His face was partly in shadow, but his small, unblinking eyes seemed to pierce into the soul. "Who are you?!" Sean screamed.

"I am the guardian of the pit," the being answered in a guttural sound. Then he took the man by the scruff of the neck and brought him to the edge of the pit and called him by name, "Sean Bradshaw," he said. "Look down. In this place of torment you should spend eternity in absolute solitude and pain that no living man is able to describe."

"No! *No!* NO!" he clamored. His mind went blank as his heart nearly burst in his chest. "Lord, save me!" he shouted.

* * *

Sweat ran off his forehead into his eyes and his mouth felt like dry cotton. He rubbed his eyes and wiped his brow. He needed water. Seconds later his mind transported him to a familiar place. He saw the steeple and the cross, then he saw the pulpit and his eyes focused on the cross hanging on the wall behind the baptistery. Then he saw himself standing in front of the pulpit, but he was younger. *I know this place!* Then a man walked up to him and put his hand on his shoulder and asked him a question. He nodded and bowed his head as the man prayed then hugged him before turning him around and making an announcement before the people sitting in the pews.

That's me! That's me when I came back from youth camp and made my confession of faith in Christ before the congregation, he realized. Then the face of the man appeared again. *That's my dad!*

Sean! Sean! he heard in his spirit. *Come back to me.* He immediately recognized the voice. *Come back to me, Sean,* he heard once more.

Then there was total blackness.

* * *

"Sean! SEAN!" he screamed. "Wake up!" He bent down and slapped his face twice. "Wake up, Sean!" George bit his lip. "Oh, God!" he exclaimed and bolted to the kitchen and splashed water into his face then carried a glass of water to Sean. "Wake up!" he shouted and threw the water into Sean's face.

Nothing.

George bit down on his index finger knuckle and scanned the room, forcing his mind to grasp the moment. He began to quiver. "What do you do now, George?" he said and started to wretch. "Think you jerk," he commanded himself. "Think!" Immediately he reached into Sean's pants and pulled out his cell phone and quickly scanned his directory to find Tiffany's number. He pressed, CALL.

"SEAN!" Tiffany answered. "Are you okay? We've been worried sick over you!"

"Tiffany, this is George Mason. I'm on your brother's phone," he said, breathing in ragged gasps. "Your brother—" he gulped in a mouthful of air, "—he's unconscious! I think he overdosed!"

* * *

FOURTEEN

"CALL 911!" Tiffany screamed into the phone. "CALL 911!"

"But Tiffany—"

"Call 911, George!" she said in fury then hissed, "If you don't—I will!"

"All right. All right" he said. "I'll call 911."

"You stay right there, you [she used a vile word]——I'm on my way over there!"

She disconnected then speed dialed her father.

* * *

Randy sat in his office across from Laurie expounding on Mike's idea of gathering a select group to pray for Sean when his cell phone chimed. He read the ID and pressed ANSWER. "DAD, SEAN HAS OVERDOSED! George called me and I ordered him to call 911! I'm on my way over to George's to wait for the police and ambulance—I'll meet you at the hospital!"

Randy jumped up from his chair and cried out, "Oh, my God!"

"What is it?!" Laurie exploded. "What's happened?"

"That was Tiffany! Sean has overdosed at George's! We need to get to the hospital right away!"

Her mind seized up in panic. She could not accept the report. It was unreal. A nightmare. Everything else was toppling down around her. Why not this too? She felt dizzy as she started to stand up. "Randy, I—" she suddenly felt faint then collapsed on the floor.

"GOD, HELP!" Randy yelled out. Second's later Susan burst through the door. "Get me some water for her—NOW!" he thundered as fear iced through him.

Susan reflexively put her hand to her mouth with her eyes fixed on Laurie lying on the floor. "LAURIE!" she shrieked.

"NOW SUSAN!" Susan rotated and ran out the door to the water cooler.

Randy rushed to Laurie and gently lifted her head off the floor. "I have you," he said softly. "You're safe. No one is going to harm you," he added as tears streamed down his face.

She rallied as he kissed her. Then he hugged and rocked her back to consciousness. Seconds later Susan brought the water. He held the cup to her mouth and said forcefully, "Take some water Laurie."

"Randy, we need to get to the hospital! I must see Sean, please!"

"I know, love, and we will go right away," he said. "As soon as you can travel."

"Help me up! "I'm ready. Let's go."

* * *

George's three cats sat pawing the front door when Tiffany arrived. She nudged them to the side then kicked the door twice. "OPEN UP, GEORGE!" she yelled. "It's Tiffany!"

The door swung open then George pointed toward the living room. "In there," he said in resignation.

Tiffany eyed him up and down with disgust and exclaimed, full of outrage, "You miserable excuse for a man! How could you be a part of this?" She pushed him out of the way and darted into the living room.

George trailed behind her until she reached Sean. Then he stood next to her and said as she kneeled down and grabbed Sean's hand, "He's still alive. He's just unconscious." Then she burst into tears and then flew into a rage. She stood erect and started punching George in the chest. "You're responsible for this! You started him on drugs! You helped him get these drugs!"

George just stood still and absorbed the punches, flinching and blinking with each blow. "I'm so sorry, Tiffany. I'm really sorry." He stepped away from her then ashamedly added, "It all started out as fun, getting high together and then when we didn't feel the high with the marijuana we upgraded to more euphoric pills but then we realized that we had to take other pills to come down to feel normal." He paused then said dolefully, "We thought we were in control and that we could stop at any time."

Tiffany swallowed hard and steeled herself. "You're sorry now? When did you graduate to shooting up? Look at his arms!" she screamed. "Is he in this condition from the drugs or dirty needles? Does it really matter?" She wiped her tears with her hands and looked back at Sean lying motionless then again at George. "You're going to burn in hell for this!"

George heard that. His eyes flashed several times. "What did you say?"

"I said you're going to burn in hell," she repeated with lesser severity. "You think doing drugs and coming down is horrible, well, let me tell you mister—" she paused and pointed her finger in his face and added, "—a thousand years from now my brother's pain will still be haunting you as you spend all eternity in total darkness separated from God!"

"Isn't that just like you Christians to defer the blame elsewhere!" he retorted. "I didn't force Sean to take the drugs, and yes, maybe I introduced him to the supplier, but he was a willing customer." He looked at her indignantly, "I didn't talk him into it Tiffany."

George started shaking then dropped to the floor next to Sean then cupped his hands on Sean's face. "Hang in there buddy! Please don't die on me. I'm sorry, Sean!" he whispered. "Can God forgive us?" he asked.

"I've never prayed before, Sean, but I'll be praying that God will help you and just maybe help me too," he said in contrition.

Tiffany heard the distant sound of the ambulance's siren as it penetrated the walls. She kneeled down next to her brother and said, "Sean, I love you. Don't leave us! Help is on the way." A strange feeling suddenly overpowered her and all the anger and hatred she felt for George was gone.

Tiffany fixed her eyes on George with a penetrating stare then extended her arm and placed her hand on his. "Do you really want God's help?" Her voice had grown softer and the venom was out of her heart so she could see George as a lost soul on his way to hell without Jesus. So who was she to judge him? She realized that while we are all sinners, Christ is the great Savior and he is no respecter of persons. Jesus does not look on the outer appearance but at the heart.

The ambulance arrived!

The EMT's rushed in with a collapsible gurney and immediately started to evaluate Sean. They placed him on the gurney then set up an IV and notified the hospital they were on the way. "George, come with me to the hospital," Tiffany said. "I want to share with you the story of God's love for you. He has a plan and a purpose for your life and you have not been living it."

"But his parents would not want me there," George objected.

"God wants you there so you can see his mercy and grace showered upon sinners," Tiffany exclaimed. "Let's go!"

"I'm ready!" he said as his eyes filled with tears of regret.

As they drove to the hospital Tiffany acknowledged that we are all responsible for our actions. She knew her brother had lost his way because how else could a Christian fall into the deception of illegal drugs. She was sure Sean was saved as she had evidenced the Holy Spirit at work in his life on many occasions.

They stopped at a traffic light. *Lord, how do I speak to this man?* She was trying to formulate the best way to communicate to George who God really is and how much he cares for his creation. "George we have a God who loves us so much," she said in deep sincerity, "that he sent his Son to die in our place. We are the ones' who broke God's laws and belong on the cross, not Jesus. But He did come and die in our place so we could spend eternity with him.

"We must acknowledge our sins and repent which means a complete turning away from them. We need to ask God to forgive us and believe that we receive the gift of the Holy Spirit to help lead, guide, and instruct us in a new direction. I'm not telling you your life will be easier because you have a long road ahead but I am telling you that it will be worth it. God's promise is that He will never leave us or forsake us. You will never be alone again."

George shook his head. "I don't think Jesus would forgive my sins—they are too many and too great."

"Is your sin greater than God's love?"

"I don't know—"

Tiffany waved him off. "You can count on God's promise in the Bible. If he says he will forgive your sin, then he will indeed, despite the size or the amount." She paused and shot a look at him and asked, "Are you ready to trust the man who died for you?"

George nodded.

They pulled into the hospital parking lot as tears ran down George's face. He turned to Tiffany and said, "How does one pray?"

Tiffany found a parking space at the emergency entrance immediately. She turned off the ignition of the car, turned to George and said, "Pray what's on your heart."

God's love and mercy were witnessed that moment when George told God how sorry he was for the path he had chosen. He had hurt so many people including his mother and father and now he wanted forgiveness and a changed life. He threw himself on God's mercy and compassion and believed. Moments later Tiffany hugged him as a brother in Christ and said in faith, "Let's tell Sean you are a new brother redeemed by the blood of your Savior."

* * *

Plantation General was the hospital all too familiar to Randy. His pastoral visitation over the years often brought him to see various church members, both young and old. But this time it was different. Much different from visiting aging members or middle age sports enthusiasts who overstretched their muscles during a workout. Yes, this time it was even much different from Tiffany's emergency surgery. This time his son's life hung in the balance from something self-inflicted.

Randy rushed through the emergency room automatic doors to see the waiting room nearly full with frantic men and women who appeared to be young to middle age. They were conversing with one another that included worried gestures.

He escorted Laurie to the intake desk and said to the duty nurse, "I'm Wilson Bradshaw. Sean Bradshaw is our son. Where is he?"

The duty nurse appeared to be agitated but keyed in the name then looked at the monitor. "He's just coming in now. He's assigned to bay 5," she said irritably.

Randy nodded then Laurie asked as she pointed to those in the waiting area, "What is going on here?"

"There has been an outbreak of the West Nile Virus here in South Florida, and their children were infected by the WNV mosquitoes while on a field trip at the Everglades Park."

"How bad?" Randy asked.

"Hopefully not too serious," the nurse replied. "The common symptoms are fever, headaches, muscle pain, vomiting and a rash. But they should be fine in several days." Randy shook his head in dismay and quickly led Laurie away into the emergency room.

"Hello Pastor Randy," he heard from behind. He turned to see a familiar face.

He scratched the side of his face and said to the nurse, "Shirley, right?"

"Right," Shirley said with a smile. Then her face grew solemn as she nodded to Laurie. "Your son is over here."

Laurie took a deep breath then squeezed Randy's hand as they walked to Sean's cubicle. When Shirley pulled back the curtain Laurie gasped and said, "Oh, my God!"

Sean had an IV in his right arm with a ventilator in his mouth. "He's not doing well at the moment," Shirley said. "We're doing a tox screen now to determine what drugs were administered."

Randy surmised that the ambulance paramedics did a preliminary diagnosis while in transit to the hospital to prepare Sean for the ER doctor. "How long?"

Shirley looked up at the wall clock. "We should have the results back in fifteen minutes."

Laurie turned to see Tiffany running down the hallway toward them. "How is he?" she exclaimed, out of breath.

As Tiffany stepped into the cubicle Laurie pointed to Sean. "We don't know yet." Then she turned to Shirley and nodded. "Shirley said it would be another fifteen minutes before we know what he took."

"Doctor?" Tiffany asked.

"Doctor Boyd, the duty ER doctor ordered the tox screen and will be back when the results are in to talk with you," Shirley advised.

An attendant walked into the cubicle and said to Shirley, "There's a Stephanie out in the waiting room who asks permission to see the patient."

Tiffany waved to the attendant. "I'll go with you." Seconds later Stephanie and Tiffany returned.

When Stephanie stepped into the cubicle and saw Sean and his family's faces, she filled up and started to weep and said through tears, "This is so terrible." Laurie walked over and put her arms around her. Tiffany, overcome with sorrow, joined them as Randy held Sean's hand.

* * *

Tiffany walked out of the ER to go check on George and give him an update on Sean. *When do I tell my parents about George? How can I tell them he came with me to the hospital and that he received the Lord when they are focused on Sean and his deliverance from the bondage of drugs? Will God give him that chance?* she wondered. "You look like you're deep in thought," she said as she approached him.

"Just thinking about Sean and my part in all of this," he replied woefully.

Tiffany could see God's spirit working on him. She would let the Spirit have free reign without commentary. "We're waiting for the results of the tox screen. When we find out, I'll come and bring you up to speed." She smiled at him and walked away. Moments passed then she felt her cell phone vibrating. She looked at the Caller ID and then shrugged her shoulders before pressing ANSWER. "Tiffany, this is Cindy Allen, Sean's friend. I was trying to reach Sean on his cell phone for the past two days but it keeps going to voice mail so I thought something was wrong. That's why I called you. Is everything okay with him?"

Tiffany vaguely remembered Sean talking about Cindy Allen as a real "sold-out" Christian in a slightly negative manner. He gave her the label, "super spiritual" and added that many of his friends said she was so spiritual she was no earthly good. "Not really," Tiffany said. "He's here in the hospital with his family."

"Hospital? What for?"

Tiffany hesitated, then: "They're doing some tests right now. We're not sure."

"I had a dream about him while I was away in Haiti on a missions trip. The Lord laid it on my heart to call him."

"We can use your prayers," Tiffany suggested. "His condition is not good."

"Where is he? I would like to see him if it's okay with your family."

At this point, Tiffany reasoned, the Bradshaw family could use all the spiritual support they can get. "We're here at Plantation General."

"I'm on my way."

* * *

Lord, you never cease to amaze me, Tiffany realized. *Your divine schedule for George to recognize his great need for you and now Cindy had a dream about Sean and wants to come and see him. Unbelievable! Yet, I believe you have a divine purpose in all of this and I also believe it will be to your glory because you are God and there is no other.*

I have to speak to Stephanie about George. We all have to help him as he is certainly going to go through withdrawals. Between my parents, Stephanie, myself, and possibly Cindy—with the help of the Lord, Sean and George will emerge on the right side of things. One thing

I know, we are not alone, you are here with us Lord! This has all been a divine appointment.

* * *

Randy sat in the corner of the cubicle reading a passage in Psalms on his phone while Laurie and Tiffany held hands at Sean's bedside. Stephanie meandered in and out of the cubicle seemingly preoccupied but Laurie knew she was in continuous prayer.

"Hello, I'm Doctor Boyd," Randy heard as the doctor walked briskly into the cubicle holding a clipboard. Stephanie followed behind him.

Randy stood up and said, "What's the diagnosis, doctor?"

"The toxicology report shows both OxyContin and Alprazolam in his system. Because of his untreated abuse of these drugs, his blood culture and echocardiogram shows he has developed acute endocarditis which is an inflammation of the inner layer of the heart, the endocardium," he replied with concern.

Randy's mind flashed back to his dream. "Oh God!"

Dr. Boyd looked at Randy. "He has been administering the OxyContin subcutaneously, under the skin, and when our lab analyzed his stomach contents we found some residue of the Alprazolam he had taken in pill form."

Laurie looked down at her son then to Doctor Boyd with pleading eyes, "What do we do now?"

Doctor Boyd nodded. "We have had good success in treating endocarditis with antibiotics if we catch it early enough," he replied with reservation.

"And—?" Tiffany said.

Doctor Boyd bit his lower lip. "This is going to be a 'wait-and-see' situation." He motioned for Laurie to sit down. "If an organism attaches to a valve surface and forms a vegetation, the host immune response is blunted. The lack of blood supply to the valves also has implications on treatment, since antibiotics have a difficulty reaching the infected valve. If the valve has been damaged the risk of bacteria attachment is increased."

Randy, with tears in his eyes asked, "Will he live, doctor?"

Doctor Boyd took a deep breath. "He's unconscious because he took an overdose, but what that has done to the brain is something we won't know until we perform an MRI this afternoon. We're waiting for some of the swelling in his brain to subside. As for your question, I believe he is strong and will pull through but—"

"But what?" Laurie said after swallowing hard.

"We could be dealing with some permanent memory loss due to brain damage," Doctor Boyd said reluctantly.

Laurie blanched and she started to wobble as her knees weakened. "Dear Jesus!" she cried out.

Randy went to her as Tiffany joined with Stephanie. They held each other as Randy looked up in the air. "Lord, you are our refuge, our fortress, and our deliverer. Save us!" he said in prayer.

"I'll check back with your later," Doctor Boyd said and walked out.

* * *

FIFTEEN

Laurie gazed out the window of the MRI waiting room into the distance then slowly turned her head to focus on the large colored print hanging on the wall. It was a copy of Claude Monet's *Woman in a Garden.* For several moments she concentrated on the woman dressed in a Redingote with a bonnet decorated with flowers and ribbons and holding a parasol while looking into the garden. Laurie wanted to transport herself into the print and imagine herself as that woman who appeared to be simply at peace with the world as she enjoyed the fullness of nature and its beauty displayed in the plethora of floral arrangements.

"Hello Mrs. Bradshaw," she heard as a young woman and her male companion walked over with Tiffany and Alex.

Laurie blinked as reality resumed its heartbreaking course to see a young woman she hardly recognized accompanied by a young man she did recognize but turned her stomach. She had made her peace with Alex but still felt she needed only her immediate family around her now. The uninvited were intruding. The young woman walked to Laurie then extended her hand. "I'm Cindy Allen, Sean's friend," she said. "When I heard about him I had to come to see him."

Tiffany nodded to her mother and said, "Alex called me on the way here and had to be with us." Then she pointed to the man standing next to Cindy. "That's George Mason."

"I know who he is," Laurie said angrily. "Why is he here?"

"He came to apologize and beg your forgiveness," Tiffany said.

Laurie shook her head and said sharply, "I don't have time for this!"

Randy walked in from the cafeteria with Stephanie and then narrowed his eyes on George. He had a passing knowledge of him through Sean, but never up close. "What are you doing here?" he said trenchantly. He walked up to him and exploded. "You have some nerve coming here!" He pointed to the exit and shouted, "Now just turn around and get out!"

George froze in place then turned to Tiffany and threw his hands up in the air as if to surrender.

Tiffany grabbed hold of Alex's hand and walked to her father. "Dad wait a minute. Thing have changed! George received Christ as his savior. He's saved!"

Laurie walked with Stephanie to Randy's side. Randy in turn took a deep breath. "Now then, George" His voice was calm, but full of menace. "I want you to answer me. What in God's name made you think that we would want you to come here?"

"Dad," Tiffany interjected, "He's really sorry."

Randy ignored her as he sibilated, "My son is on the verge of death and if he lives he could have brain damage, and you come here to salve your conscience saying that *you got saved* and are sorry? This sounds like a fox-hole confession if ever I heard one." Laurie put her arms around her husband and hugged him, saying nothing. He nodded and said gruffly, "Speak up, George! Let me hear your side of things."

George looked around to each of the bystanders then began to sweat profusely. Randy assumed it was withdrawals. Then George began to weep. "Mr. Bradshaw, I came to see Sean, that's part of it. But I knew I would have to face you and his mother, and that is something that I need to do as well." He buried his face in his hands then looked up at both Randy and Laurie. "I beg your forgiveness."

Laurie squeezed Randy's hand and said, "What should we do?"

Randy stepped back in silence. Yes, it was up to him, he thought. He knows he is a pastor and an ambassador for Christ but he is also a father and his son is in critical condition right now. Intellectually he knows George is not responsible for Sean, a bad influence definitely, but Satan, the god of this world is the real enemy who entices young people with the thrill of abandonment from all responsibility through drugs.

These young people never think of addiction or consequences but soon enough they are held in bondage to the drugs and their lives start to spiral out of control.

He shook his head and in so doing, his eyes caught sight of a bracelet on Alex's wrist. He recognized it immediately: *WWJD. Yeah*, he thought, *what would Jesus do?* Finally, "I'm not sure where that leaves us," he said to Laurie.

"Pastor Bradshaw," George said in desperation. "I need to tell you something, and I'm hoping you'll understand me a little more."

Randy nodded. "Go on."

He swallowed hard then steeled himself to lucidity. "I see that you and your family have a deep, caring relationship with Sean. Your family has shown its love for him by your actions. You have done everything possible to pull him out of this pit he's in, and I see that clearly." He paused as his eyes began to water and his voice grew weaker. Randy recognized the tears and the meekness of spirit. "In my life," he explained, "I rejected my parents as they reached out to help me. In my extreme selfishness I ran away taking my grandfather's inheritance to me for school and squandered it on drugs, alcohol and parties.

"My parents loved me, my grandmother adored me and I didn't care about them. I only cared about George and what he wanted. I have hurt them deeply and perhaps irreparably but just in the few short hours that I have responded to Jesus' call I see my sin and the damage it has inflicted on my family. I may never get the chance to ask for their forgiveness but I'm standing before you now asking for yours."

Randy heard his story. Laurie looked up at him and said, "Randy, we have to help him."

Randy's heart sank. He couldn't ignore George's plea for help and his apparent desire to change. It had to be real. He looked over at Tiffany and Alex, then around to Stephanie and Cindy. They were watching him carefully. He turned and left Laurie and George momentarily and walked toward the door then came to a halt. The parable of the lost sheep suddenly came to mind: *…if a man owns a hundred sheep, and one of them wanders away, will he not leave the ninety-nine on the hills and go to look for the one that wandered off? And if* *he finds it, …he is happier about that one sheep than about the ninety-nine that did not wander off. In the same way your Father in heaven is not willing that any of these little one should be lost.* He turned around and walked up to George and threw his arms around him. "I forgive you," he said.

When he looked at Laurie and Tiffany and the others, they were all crying.

* * *

Doctor Boyd entered the MRI waiting room with the results of the MRI scan. He looked at the family and said, "While I cannot see any damage to the brain at this time I am very concerned that the brain is still very swollen and your son remains unconscious. We will administer mild sedatives to keep him at rest and antibiotics for the heart but it is a wait-and-see scenario. Certainly I will keep you advised of any changes."

"When can we see him?" Laurie asked.

"They're bringing him up to ICU now," Doctor Boyd said. "So give them 30 minutes or so before you join him. I've conferred with Doctor Percy who treated your daughter a while back and he will look in on Sean later today."

*   *   *

Randy and Laurie entered ICU to be with their son. Laurie kept her eyes focused on her boy hooked up to all the medical diagnostic paraphernalia monitoring his vitals. "He looks peaceful," Laurie said as she touched his cheek and rubbed his arm hoping for a response. Without warning a flood of tears overwhelmed her as her heart ached over this son she loved so much. Again and again her mind tormented her with thoughts of failure. What could she have done differently? *Please Lord, give us another chance to love and care for Sean*, she entreated her spirit.

Randy himself was deep in thought about his son. He wondered what was going through his mind at this time or was he really at peace resting in a sedative-induced calmness. He prayed that the Lord he loved would see fit to return Sean to them without brain damage. *Lord, you can reach our Sean in the state that he's in. Forgive him, Lord, heal him Father, equip and enable him for your divine use.*

Dr. Percy walked into ICU interrupting Randy and Laurie's thoughts. "Good to see you again, but unfortunately not under the best of circumstances." He looked at Randy and Laurie and said, "I know your dealing with a lot right now with Sean's MRI results and his acute endocarditis, but there is something else. We suspect an abnormality in his liver functions. Hopefully that will not exacerbate his problems."

Laurie clutched Randy's hand. "Is that serious?"

"It can be," Doctor Percy replied with concern. "I've ordered a liver enzyme test which is a group of tests that detect inflammation and damage to the liver. Because of his abuse of drugs, we have to be sure. We'll have to wait-and-see."

Randy had heard the 'wait-and-see' response before and it was always ominous when it came to medical emergencies. "How long before we know, doctor?"

"The total evaluation of all these tests takes 24-48 hours before we receive the findings and come to a complete diagnosis."

We have to hold our breath once more until we find out, Randy thought as he nodded. "Thanks doc," he said as Doctor Percy walked out.

"It is time to leave," the nurse announced. "We have to change his linens and take care of his hygiene."

Randy nodded reluctantly then joined hands with Laurie as he prayed for their son. Then they both told Sean how much they loved him and walked out to rejoin the rest of their family. As they walked out of ICU they were brought to tears to see so many members of their congregation along with the deacons on their knees in the waiting room praying for their pastor's son and family.

* * *

Lester, along with Mike Rice and Rick Kelly, were the first to approach Randy and Laurie in front of the rest of the group. Lester being the designated spokesperson said, "Pastor Randy, we have been in prayer and your staff," he paused to nod to the other four congregants, "along with these folks here, believe we need to bring this family crisis of yours before the congregation. After all, we are *all* family."

Laurie traded looks with Randy. *Is it time to bring the church into this family secret?* Laurie thought. *Do they need to know about Sean's drug overdose? Is this going to cost Randy the pastorate?*

Randy lived with Laurie long enough to know how she thinks. He could read her. *It's time; we have nowhere else to turn. We must trust the Lord for the outcome.* He smiled at Lester after giving Laurie the nod. "Yes, we need to do that right away."

Mike walked up to him. "Pastor, you and Laurie need to get some rest. We'll stay here and keep watch while you and Laurie go home for a while."

"Right," Randy said. But first he had to do something. He walked away from his deacons and up to George sitting in the waiting room. "George, I need to speak to you. George stood up followed him out into the corridor.

"Everything okay, Mr. Bradshaw?"

Randy leaned up against the wall then placed his hand on George's shoulder. "George, I feel compelled to tell you that you face a difficult road ahead to rid yourself of your past and that you're going to need as much help as you can get."

George signaled his assent. "Did you have something in mind?"

"I think it a good idea that we bring your family back into your life. You said you were estranged from them, but now that you've made your peace with God, I believe the Lord would want you to make your peace with your parents."

"But how—?"

Randy waved him off. "I want your permission to call them as your pastor and tell them what's happened."

George shook his head. "Pastor Randy, I think they've given up on me. I doubt your call would mean very much to them."

"Let's not rule out that the Lord is in control, George, and that the bible says we have been given the ministry of reconciliation. That means that we have to try. The rest is up to the Lord."

George's shoulders rose and fell. "If you believe God is leading you, who am I to disagree?"

Randy took that the response from this new Christian as a *yes*. "Give me their phone number."

* * *

"Rats!" Randy said as he closed his phone. Frederick and Elizabeth Mason were not available the message machine dictated. *Leave a message*, it instructed. So Randy left the message that their son, George, was in Florida and that as his pastor, they should call him. *That's all I can do, Lord.*

Randy walked back into the waiting room and gestured to George who quickly went to him. "Left a message for them to call me on my cell phone."

George sighed and frowned. "You tried, right."

"I'm sure they'll call me," Randy asserted and then waved to Laurie to follow him out the door. Laurie passed instructions to Tiffany to call her the moment Sean became conscious.

* * *

Randy fought off the relentless thoughts of failure all the way home. His failure as a father and failure as a pastor was increasingly on his heart. The battle against slipping into the slough of despond over Sean and the impact his addiction problem would have on his family and the ministry at times seemed overwhelming. He knew Laurie felt the same way. But the responsibility of leading his family to the foot of the cross and leaving the burden there was his and his alone. But that didn't make it any easier.

"I'll put on the coffee," Laurie said as they walked into the house.

Redeemed how I love to proclaim it, his cell phone sang out. He grabbed his phone and checked the CALLER ID. The call was from out of the area. "Pastor Randy," he answered.

"Mr. Bradshaw, this is Fred Mason, George's father," the caller announced.

"Oh, yes," Randy began. "Thanks for returning my call." Randy gestured to Laurie and mouthed *Fredrick Mason* to her. She nodded and walked into the kitchen.

Mason cleared his throat and said, "This is a difficult call for us since we haven't heard from or about George in two years. Is he all right?"

Randy thought he heard his voice cracking as if he were very upset. "Yes, he's all right. In fact, he's doing quite well right now, Mr. Mason. I asked George for permission to call you and give you some good news. First, like I mentioned on your answering machine he's down here with us in Plantation, Florida, and he has had a major turnaround in his life, and as his pastor I wanted to call you and let you know. Secondly, that turnaround came about because he turned his life over to Christ."

"Him being in Florida explains why we haven't been able to find him here in Maine," Mason explained. "And as far as his turnaround goes, that sounds like a good thing, Pastor Randy."

"Yes, that is a *very* good thing," Randy said. "But there is a down side to his turnaround that I needed to discuss with you."

"Oh. What's that?"

"This is the hard part, Mr. Mason," Randy ventured. "You see, your son has been heavily involved in drugs and now that he's made a decision for Christ, he wants to stay clean. And besides that, he expressed a desire to make things right with his parents. But this is going to be a difficult road even with him going to rehab. So as his pastor I'm asking you if you will come to Florida and help him through the first stages of his recovery." He paused then added, "I also believe you're coming here will go a long way in bringing reconciliation to your family."

Silence.

"What about us bringing him up here to Maine?" Mason said.

"Well, the problem with that, Mr. Mason, is that George was doing drugs with my son, Sean, and Sean is now in the hospital from an overdose, and George feels somewhat responsible. I believe he wants to stay here in Florida until Sean is back on his feet once again."

"Oh, I see," Mason said dolefully. "Can you hold on?"

"Of course."

Moments passed.

"I checked with his mother," Mason said, "and we will make the earliest flight arrangements to Florida." He choked up. "Please tell George that we love him and want to help him."

Randy's spirit soared! "I will be sure to tell him that. We look forward to seeing you real soon." Suddenly he began to see a glimpse of God's big picture of rebuilding out of chaos. Moments later he excitedly told Laurie the good news then phoned Tiffany at the hospital to explain to George about his talk with his father. He added that both him and Laurie wanted George to stay with them until his parents arrived. That's when Alex volunteered to accompany him as a shield against the Evil One. Randy thought it a grand gesture.

* * *

Two hours later, Randy received a call from the hospital. Sean had slipped into a coma.

* * *

SIXTEEN

Laurie carefully held Sean's hand then began to stroke it trying to invoke a response, but it was not meant to be. His body remained still with the exception of his chest rising and falling with the aid of a ventilator. Randy watched Sean's monitor and noticed what he thought was a regular heartbeat, not fully understanding what happens when a person is in a coma. Does one think when in a coma? Dream? Nightmare? He didn't know. He only knew that when he looked down at his son lying in this comatose state that he could only shake his head and cry.

"Mr. Bradshaw," Doctor Percy interrupted Randy's thoughts.

Randy blinked. "What happened to him?"

Doctor Percy addressed both Randy and Laurie. "We're not sure how this unfortunate turn of events unfolded, but we are going to do another MRI of his brain within the hour. Just in case we missed something."

"Is this thing necessary?" Laurie asked, pointing to the ventilator.

"Yes," Doctor Percy replied. "His breathing was very erratic. Hopefully we will not need tracheal intubation if his condition worsens, but let's hope for the best."

The possibility of Sean needing a flexible plastic tube into his trachea to maintain an open airway was more than she could handle as this point. "May those words go from your lips to God's ears," she said sorrowfully and sat down next to Sean's bed.

"I'm going down to the waiting room to advise all the others what's going on," Randy said, his breath nearly catching in his throat. *I need to get out of here.*

Laurie nodded woefully. "I'll keep watch."

* * *

Forty-five minutes passed before Randy returned to Sean's room, his resolve steadfast. Tomorrow, Sunday, he would go before the congregation and explain everything then hold a prayer vigil. Leaving the outcome with God.

"I'll be standing next to you," Laurie said after he told her his plan.

A threefold cord is not quickly broken, he thought. "Tiffy said she would join us too."

* * *

As Randy walked into the half-filled sanctuary he sensed the atmosphere of the congregation was subdued. *News travels fast*, he realized, *especially in the church*. What his church family knew about his son and the steps leading up to his hospitalization was either unknown or very limited, but that was part of his mission today: to set things right by stating the facts, even if it meant polarization.

He walked in and sat down next to Laurie then surveyed the pews as they began to fill up, noticing most of his staff was present, all but his faithful deacon, Lester, who volunteered to stand watch over Sean.

Laurie poked him in his side. "Randy, look," she whispered, "George is here and he must've brought his parents along."

Randy turned to see George along with a man and woman in their 50s meandering into the sanctuary, looking for an open space in a pew. Randy stood up and walked over to them.

"Pastor Randy," George said gleefully as he nodded toward the couple, "these are my parents, Fred and Elizabeth Mason. They were looking forward to meeting you so I invited them to your church." Randy extended a warm welcome to them as other members of the congregation looked on with expansive smiles. He smiled within himself after recognizing another small glimpse that God was up to something special once again: rebuilding out of chaos.

*   *   *

Knowing that his pastor was about to make an important announcement, Rick carefully selected Christian hymns that would convey to the congregation a sense of worship, humility, and especially forgiveness, starting off with

There Is a Fountain and ending with *To God Be the Glory*.

Mike then ascended the pulpit and publically prayed aloud for God's blessing on the Word of God, then invited Pastor Randy to give the sermon.

Randy carried his bible with him to the pulpit then opened it to the book of First John chapter one, verse nine, and read, "'If we confess our sins, he is faithful and just and will forgive us our sins and purify us from al unrighteousness'." He began to choke up, then cleared his throat and said, "I have to make a confession before my church family today. God has shown me that I have not been the testimony nor have I been the witness I should be as your pastor.

"Over the past year I have allowed my pride to dictate my behavior and I reveled in the growth of this ministry that included our new building and in many ways this pride has blinded me to what my real calling should be: To be your pastor. I have slipped into a pit where I have acted more like a business manager than a shepherd. Yes, I have attended to my duties as a minister, but in my heart, I have allowed my pride to concentrate more on church growth than on individual spiritual growth in the lives of God's people.

"I believe that the Lord was displeased with my actions and because of this He brought calamity and trials into my family—" he paused and shot a look at Laurie. She nodded to give her approval. When he scanned the congregation he could see many were whispering to each other. *Go on, Randy,* he said to himself. *Go on!*

"To those who may have heard rumors or to those *in the know,* I need to explain our family crisis." He swallowed hard, and then exhaled deeply. "My son has a serious drug addiction problem and is now in a coma at Plantation General from what we believe is an overdose." He moaned in his spirit than began to whimper. "Both Laurie and I, along with Tiffany and our church leadership are heartbroken over this—" he stopped abruptly to wipe his tears with his handkerchief. He bit his lower lip and continued. "To a degree I hold myself responsible for this since God views me as the protective spiritual umbrella over my family. I believe the Lord wanted to break me of my sin of pride since I have kept my so-called 'private' affairs from the church when I should have allowed you as my church family to be a part of my own family by asking you to pray about our problems. We are not immune from them. Yes, we too have problems in our family." He paused to see Laurie and Tiffany walking up to the pulpit then they stood on both sides of him. When Laurie looked into the congregation in front of her, most of them were crying.

Tiffany spotted George when he stood up and started walking to the pulpit. She tapped her father on the shoulder and whispered to him, "Dad, George is coming up. Should I wave him off?"

'No, let him be," he whispered back. Randy waited until George reached the pulpit as the congregation exchanged soft murmurs expressing their surprise and curiosity. Once he arrived, Randy pulled him between Tiffany and himself and said, "It has been said that every cloud has a silver lining. Well, if there is any good that has come out of our family crisis so far, it has been George Mason." Through a strained smile he put his arm around George and added, "George, once bound up in addiction along with Sean, has found new freedom in Christ. George has committed his life to Christ and I pray you will welcome him into our church family." Many of the church members jumped to their feet and started clapping. Laurie started crying. She took their acceptance as tacit approval of Randy's confession.

Randy looked at Frederick and Elizabeth as they held back their tears. "I have come before our church family to ask your forgiveness," he continued in his plea, "and humbly ask you to enter into prayer for our son."

Mike quickly stepped onto the worship platform and held up a microphone. "My friends and fellow Christians," he said, his voice vibrating with intensity, "we need to do more than pray for our pastor during this emergency. He is a man of God who has served us well in this church and has been severely humbled and so we need to hold his family up and enter into a period of prayer *and* fasting!"

Without warning, Cindy walked up to the worship platform next to Mike then nodded to Tiffany. Seconds later she rolled up her blouse sleeves as Mike unwittingly handed her the microphone. "I used to be a drug addict!" she announced. "I've rolled up my sleeves so you can see the scars of both the track marks and the slash marks on my wrists from where I attempted to commit suicide six years ago."

"Oh, my God!" Tiffany said numbly. "I never knew that."

"Neither did I," Randy said.

"But God in his grace saved me," Cindy continued. "Even though I was in a drug stupor, he called me to himself and I have been living for him ever since. After one year of therapy and a strong commitment to a prayer partner, to this day, I am clean!" Then she turned to Randy and Laurie. "I wanted you to know that God is still in the miracle business and that he will do the same for Sean and George!"

Laurie bust into tears and hugged Cindy. "Bless you!" she cried out. Tiffany and George walked to her and joined them.

George's parents hastily stepped into the aisle and walked to the platform and within minutes the congregation—led by the Van Flemings—flowed out of the pews and rushed to their side and embraced them.

They were all one family now and there would be no more secrets.

SEVENTEEN

Renewed by the overwhelming expression of the church's acceptance, Randy and Laurie returned to the hospital with Tiffany following in her own car with Alex. Their spirits were flying high but it would be short lived.

"Expecting a change?" Laurie asked Randy as they both set eyes on Sean. He lay motionless in the same position as before with the medical apparatus attached to him raising their level of concern.

Randy shrugged his shoulders. "I guess so," he said, then corrected himself. "Perhaps I'm being a bit presumptuous in expecting the Lord to fix the problem on my schedule."

Laurie said nothing. She just hugged him and said, "In His time."

Moments later Tiffany and Alex arrived. They too showed signs of disappointment.

Doctor Percy walked in behind them and then walked to Sean's monitor and pressed several buttons to measure any changes then checked his ventilator. His breathing appeared to improve. "We have the results of the latest MRI and find that Sean's brain is still swollen but apart from that we cannot find anything unusual. We are puzzled as to why he remains unconscious. However, the good news is that his liver functions are no longer in the red zone and that is promising."

"Thank you, Jesus," Laurie mouthed to Randy.

"We will do more tests in the morning," Doctor Percy said and walked out.

Waves of doubt suddenly washed over Randy's heart. Laurie knew him long enough to read his mind. "God is working, Randy," she said. "We must trust him."

Randy looked over at Tiffany and Alex who watched him carefully. "I know you're right," he reminded himself and saw his daughter and Alex smile.

Moments later the duty nurse walked into the room and removed the ventilator. "Doctor Percy's orders," she said.

Laurie blinked and then nodded. *Praise the Lord!*

Two hours passed in vigilance with the family simply praying among themselves. Then...

"Dad, look!" Tiffany exclaimed as she pointed, "I just saw Sean open one eye!"

Randy and Laurie stepped to Sean's bedside and clutched his hand. "Sean, it's mom and dad!"

No response.

Tiffany walked over and starting patting his forehead as Alex looked on. "We love you, Sean."

He moved his head from side to side momentarily. "Sean! We're here!" Randy exclaimed.

Sean's forehead started to perspire profusely. Then: "Where am I?" he said in a low whisper as his eyes slowly opened.

"You're in Plantation General," Laurie said.

He started to raise his head off the pillow. "Sean, stay still," Tiffany said, controlling her voice.

He fell back into the pillow and squeezed his eyes shut. "God help me!" he cried out and began to thrash in the bed.

"Get the nurse!" Laurie directed Tiffany. Tiffany rotated and dashed to the nurse's station.

"I'M FALLING!" Sean screamed. "HELP ME!"

"Nurse!" Randy yelled, "Help!"

Laurie and Tiffany rubbed his arm as his eyes opened as if he were in a trance. "Where am I?" he cried out.

"He's delirious," the nurse said as she rushed to check his vital signs then turned to Randy and said, "I'll call the doctor stat to prescribe something to calm him down," and bolted out the door.

Sean riveted his eyes on Randy then grabbed him by the shirt and shouted, "I'M IN A PLACE WHERE NO ONE RETURNS. YOU HAVE TO HELP ME!"

"RANDY!" Laurie shrieked, "DO SOMETHING!"

"THERE'S NO BOTTOM!" Sean bellowed.

"He's having a nightmare about hell!" Randy realized.

"RANDY!" Laurie repeated, "DO SOMETHING, NOW!"

Randy nodded and placed his hand on Sean's head and then looked up and cried aloud, "By the blood of the Lord Jesus, I command all demonic agents to cease harassing Sean!"

Sean suddenly went inert. "He's calming down," Laurie said.

Then: "I see the cross," Sean whispered in wonder. "It's the cross of Jesus!"

Randy shook his head in shock and took two steps back. *My dream of the cemetery! He's living out my dream, my nightmare where he dies! Oh, God!*

"What's all this?!" Doctor Percy exclaimed as he abruptly reappeared in the room, the duty nurse in his shadow. He took one look at Sean and then at his monitor. His heart rate was spiking and his blood pressure falling rapidly.

"Doctor Percy, do something!" Laurie boomed.

Doctor Percy's mouth dropped open as he gaped at the monitor, deciding what to do.

Sean's arms began to shake and his head rocked back and forth then his eyes flashed open and he went still once again. "I'm safe now," he said in a low whisper. "I'm safe with Jesus."

Laurie reflexively covered her mouth with her hand. "He's dying Randy!" she cried out.

Doctor Percy motioned to the nurse and ordered a shot of Diazepam. The nurse bolted out the door and returned within thirty seconds with the hypodermic needle in hand. She shot a look at Doctor Percy who gestured his approval.

Then: Sean bolted upright in the bed. "Hold it!" Doctor Percy said with a halting motion.

Sean's eyes scanned the room then focused on his father. "Don't worry dad, I'm okay."

* * *

"Sean!" Randy reached out for Sean but he had already closed his eyes and seemed lifeless.

Doctor Percy immediately checked his pulse. "He's unconscious, but out of the coma. We will set up another MRI to see if there is any lessening of brain activity."

Randy, Laurie, Tiffany and Alex were speechless, scared, and confused. *What just happened?*

As if prompted by God's Spirit, Randy started to cry and praise God for he took this episode as a hopeful sign that Sean was going to recover. "We don't know how much a person can hear while unconscious or in a coma, but we have just witnessed a battle in Sean's life where it seems to me that Jesus was the victor!" Dr. Percy nodded as if what Randy said made perfect sense and then walked out to order the new MRI.

* * *

A few hours later the Bradshaw's received their first good news since this nightmare began. The MRI revealed that the swelling of Sean's brain was reducing and the doctors had every hope that he would come into consciousness at any time. Everyone wanted to be there when this happened; however, the doctor could not predict whether it would be hours or days. "Let us rejoice in what we do know," Randy exclaimed happily. "The rest we will leave in God's hands."

"I'm with you." A familiar voice intruded into their praise. It was Stephanie.

Almost in one accord they said, "Where have you been?"

"I have never left you without my prayers but you have been through so much I thought I would do some investigating for you. You see, I truly believed that the Lord would bring Sean through because He has a plan for his life. Sometimes we have to go through some dark waters to finally get to that plan and I should know from experience. Knowing that Sean would need some rehabilitation and counseling I found a place that I think you will be happy to bring him to. I wanted to take some of the pressure off you both and there is such a difference in some of the places and the programs that are out there I needed to do some heavy research for you. *Second Chance* is the name of the place that looks like the right place for Sean. Christians founded it and the programs are all Bible-based leading the patient to recognize that apart from God we can do nothing. The doctors are all licensed and the nurses are all certified." She paused and smiled. "Do I hear rejoicing?"

Randy led them all to Stephanie. They threw their arms around her telling her how grateful they were to

have such a loyal friend. They shared with her their hope
for Sean's full recovery and thanked her for finding a
place for Sean to heal and rediscover the power of God.
"We expect Sean to regain consciousness at any time
now, so we are taking turns staying with him so that when
he awakes one of us will be with him," Randy advised.

* * *

Resplendent sunshine showered through Sean's hospital
room window the following afternoon. *It was a good
sign*, Randy thought. *Light was overpowering darkness.
Yeah, that's the message of the gospel.* He turned to Sean
and bowed his head in prayer for him.

Sean unexpectedly opened his eyes to see his
father's bended head. Immediately thoughts entered his
heart. *How many times have I seen my father just like this
praying for someone or something? How many times?
Can't count them. I know he's been in deep prayer for me
now—I can feel the heat of his prayers and petitions on
my behalf.* "I'm sorry Dad," he said.

Randy lifted his head and replied, "I'm sorry too
since I wasn't there for you when you needed me most.

But God be praised because He has returned you to us and to the divine purpose He has for you."

"Dad, Jesus spoke to me or at least I think he did while I was unconsciousness. He said He did not create me for the life I was living and that He does have a plan for me. But I was terrified and thought it was a nightmare."

"It was a nightmare," Randy said staring at him, "and I had a similar one a few weeks ago but in my nightmare I lost you. God is so gracious to us and as we acknowledge our weaknesses, we gain His strength." He sighed and added, "Sean, I just want you to know that your mom, sister, and I are here for you every step of the way. If that wasn't enough, the church is fasting and praying for your complete healing but most importantly that the Lord says He will never leave your or forsake you."

"I feel so tired, dad, and my eyes are so very heavy."

"Go to sleep, Sean, and when you awake your mother and sister will be here."

"Dad for the first time since you prayed with me before I went to sleep as a child, I feel safe."

"Sean, sleep on. You are safe."

* * *

It was evening time and songs of praise filled Sean's hospital room. Randy and Laurie likened it to a family reunion of sorts while Tiffany and Alex acted like they were holding a worship service on Sean's behalf.

The color was returning to Sean's face and it did not seem that he had suffered any permanent brain damage. After the initial tears of joy, Sean asked, "What's with George?"

Randy's eyes lit up with delight.

Sean was curious. "What gives dad?"

"The Bible says that 'all things work together for good' and your friend George made a profession of faith in Christ and has been reunited with his parents. He has a long road ahead of him as you do, but he is going to make it because our Lord makes beauty out of ashes."

Sean's filled up with tears. He could barely respond. "Where is George now? Can I see him?"

"Of course," Randy replied. "He asked when he could come along with your friend Cindy Allen who has been a real prayer warrior for you as well."

* * *

The morning sunlight seemed to really brighten Sean's room. He felt even stronger and his duty nurse said it was time for him to get out of the bed and get some light exercise. After several attempts to stand without feeling faint, he managed to walk to the chair and sit down. He was amazed that he was so weak but the nurse assured him he would feel better and stronger each day.

He managed to eat a little breakfast and complete a sponge bath but fatigue set in and a morning nap was in order. "Ahh!" he exclaimed as he hit the fresh sheets on the bed. It felt so good and his heart was full of thanksgiving. Within moments he dozed off.

* * *

Noontime brought George and his parents to the hospital. George was profusely sweating despite the cool, dry outdoor temperature. The continual sweating and anxiety were symptoms of withdrawal that were increasingly becoming problematic for him.

As he walked into Sean's room both men's eyes filled with tears. "We have both been saved from the destruction of both our minds and our bodies you know," Sean stated as George and his parents entered the hospital room.

"How well I know," George replied. "It is so good to see you man, you had us all pretty scared." He turned and with a sweeping motion added, "Sean, this is my Mom and Dad, Fred and Elizabeth Mason. We have been estranged for over two years but receiving Jesus caused me to realize how I was wasting my life and how much I have hurt the people I loved the most. They have come to take me home to Maine where I will enter a rehab for a while. Initially I was going to stay in Florida but I have been apart from my family for so long and I need their support. We leave tonight for home. We were waiting to see how God was going to answer our prayers concerning you."

Fred Mason displayed a grateful expression then said, "We are very glad to meet you Sean and even happier that your doctors feel you can experience full recovery."

"I'm only sorry we cannot take the time to get to know you better" George's mom chimed in. "But as you can probably see George needs to get some medical attention. I truly hope you will come visit us in Maine when you are able because you will always be welcome."

Sean was very touched and responded to them sincerely when he assured them that he was looking forward to what God had in mind for both of their lives. Whenever the time was right, he would make a trip to Maine.

"Hey, let's not get too melancholy on my last day in Florida. We'll keep in touch and I'll leave you the number of *The Sanctuary* where I will be staying," George noted.

"Right" Sean replied, then affirmed, "We will both keep in touch but better still we can pray for each other for God's power and strength to get us through the next couple of months."

Mr. and Mrs. Mason gently intruded and reminded George that they still had to pack and return the rented car before their flight back to Maine. After an emotional goodbye, George and his parents left the hospital.

* * *

Sean sat in his chair contemplating what comes next and when he was going to be transferred to Second Chance, a rehab his parents had decided on for him. It's not that he didn't want to go because he knew he needed to get help but he was full of anxiety and fear of failure. He had already made such a mess of things and what if he couldn't do it? Perhaps he would fall into the temptation of drugs again. What if his whole life was a series of failures?

Moments after his brief journey into disbelief and he was really feeling sorry for himself, Cindy Allen walked in carrying a huge bear with a lot of bandages covering his furry body. "What's that?" Sean asked.

"Nice to see you too" replied Cindy. This is *Boo Boo Bear*. He's been pretty beat up but now that he's been wrapped and cleaned up, his wounds will start to heal. He's on his way to recovery just as you are. I thought a little visual aid might help when doubts creep in so I brought *Boo Boo Bear* to keep you company."

"Well you must have read my mind," Sean replied. "I guess I was just filling my head with doubts and fears of complete recovery."

"You might be wondering why you haven't seen your family yet today," Cindy said. "I asked them for some time alone with you so I could share something with you. They knew George and his parents were coming to say goodbye so they told me to tell you they will be here later."

"What is so important that you want to share it with me in private?" Sean asked.

"I wanted to tell you face to face that I have already stood before your church family and told them about me."

"This is getting interesting, please go on," Sean cheered.

"They say a picture is worth a thousand words and even a thousand words would not be enough to praise the Lord for his mercy extended to me," Cindy said in wonder as she started to tear up. Then she proceeded to roll up the sleeves of her shirt revealing the evidence of her drug addiction. "Sean, God saved me from myself.

He did for me what I could not do alone and He is there for you as well." Tears rolled down her cheeks.

Sean was stunned. He was speechless. *This can't be. Not Cindy Allen, Miss Christianity, the devout churchgoer and bold witness for Jesus.* Sean finally found his voice and said, "I really don't know what to say, and I never knew or expected this."

"Sean, my motive in telling you this is to encourage you that failure is never final with Jesus. Just look at me," Cindy cried softly. "I want to be here for you and help you through the process of recovery because it is a daily struggle to get the drugs out of your system and your mind," she reasoned. "You have a loving God and wonderful parents and a church family all praying for you. Since I have walked this path before, I thought you could lean on me and I'll try to explain to you what to expect in the days to come."

"I'm overwhelmed after all God has done for me and I'm so grateful for George receiving Jesus and now I have you stepping in as a friend to help me. It is so much more than I deserve," Sean sobbed.

"None of us deserve the grace that was bestowed on us at salvation nor the righteousness of Jesus that was imputed to us but the Lord has filled the void in my life and I want my life to honor Him," admitted Cindy.

"I want that too," acknowledged Sean.

"Then let's help each other to accomplish the task that God has set before us. Do you agree?" asked Cindy.

"Agreed!" Sean said with a broad smile.

* * *

Moments after Cindy left he turned aside then spent some time praying and reading his Bible. He encouraged himself in the Lord and he felt the peace that surpasses understanding surround him. He believed that he had God's protection, provision, peace, and most of all His presence to help him overcome whatever the future had waiting for him. "It is going to be a great day," he whispered to himself.

* * *

Randy, Laurie, and Tiffany arrived at the hospital in late afternoon and found Sean in a very calm and serene state of mind. "I want to tell you how much I love you and how sorry I am for the heartache I've caused you," Sean said in somber tones. "I am ready to go to Second Chance because I believe God is giving me a second chance," he added.

Randy nodded in appreciation. "I think God is giving our family a second chance to love Him and serve Him with a pure heart, to love one another, to be there for each other, to pray for one another and to have no more secrets from each other."

"Hallelujah!" They all said in unison.

* * *

EPILOGUE

One year later we find Plantation Gate Church thriving with new members who have flocked to find Pastor Randy to be a shepherd that is transparent and authentic. He has become the pastor so many desire to serve under. His testimony of love and forgiveness is so needed in our dark world. His messages about the Cross of Grace and Mercy draws hungry and thirsty souls to seek the Savior.

Sean is coming home today from Second Chance and Randy, Laurie, and Tiffany have been looking forward to this day with great joy. Sean bloomed and grew under the teaching at Second Chance. He studied and read and gave small group Bible studies. His mentors told Randy not to be surprised if Sean decided to seek the pastorate in the future. For now, their family had so much to praise the Lord about.

A year ago the Bradshaw family was a mess, the church was in danger of going in the wrong direction but God in His infinite mercy turned everything around to His glory and honor. *The Bradshaw's would have it no other way.*

Tiffany was especially anxious for Sean to come home because she and Alex had put off their wedding until Sean could be a part of their happiness. In two weeks Tiffany and Alex would be married and start their new life together as missionaries to the Navajo Indians in Northeastern Arizona. Both Tiffany and Alex had spent the last year studying the ways and the history of the Navajo tribe along with their unique language. The Navajo have a religious system that incorporates many gods with supernatural powers. As a people, they are religious believing in good and evil. The work ahead for Alex and Tiff will be both exciting and challenging.

* * *

Laurie, Tiffany, and Stephanie peered out the window until finally Randy pulled the car into the driveway. They all ran out to greet and welcome Sean home. The group family hug exuded joyous tears! Sean appreciated being home and was delighted to see Cindy Allen in the living room standing under the WELCOME HOME SEAN banner. She had visited Sean often at Second Chance and it is safe to say they had become more than friends. Sean and Cindy were more like soul mates.

This was a real party with many of the families from Plantation Gate Church in attendance. As Sean was making the rounds greeting everyone, he received a phone call from George. "Welcome home buddy" George said exuberantly.

"It is wonderful to be home" Sean sighed.

"What are your plans, Sean?" George wanted to know.

"Right now I am going back to school here at home. I want the Lord to confirm in my heart his plans for me so I'll take it one day at a time," Sean explained.

"Wouldn't have anything to do with that cute little Cindy would it?" George teased.

"I'm hoping she will be a part of my future," Sean stated boldly. "What about you?"

"I'm off to Bible College, can you believe it? Me! George Mason in Bible College? We certainly worship a God of miracles because I am one of his miraculous healings," George said in awe.

"God bless you and keep in touch, brother" Sean encouraged.

"Coming right back at you friend!" George replied.

* * *